Medea

By Christa Wolf

NAN A. TALESE

Doubleday

New York   London   Toronto   Sydney   Auckland

Medea
A Modern Retelling

Christa Wolf

Translated from the German by John Cullen

F
WOL

PUBLISHED BY NAN A. TALESE
an imprint of Doubleday
a division of Bantam Doubleday Dell Publishing Group, Inc.
1540 Broadway, New York, New York 10036

DOUBLEDAY is a trademark of Doubleday, a division of
Bantam Doubleday Dell Publishing Group, Inc.

Book design by Maria Carella

The publication of this book has been supported by Inter Nationes.

Library of Congress Cataloging-in-Publication Data
Wolf, Christa.
   Medea: a modern retelling / Christa Wolf: translated from the German
   by John Cullen. — 1st U.S. ed.
      p.   cm.
   I. Title.
PT2685.036M413   1998
833'.914—dc21   97–24274
                              CIP

ISBN 0-385-49060-7
Copyright © 1996 by Luchterhand Literaturverlag GmbH
Translation copyright © 1998 by John Cullen
All Rights Reserved
Printed in the United States of America
April 1998
First Edition in the United States of America
10 9 8 7 6 5 4 3 2 1

Achronism is not the inconsequential juxtaposition
of epochs, but rather their interpenetration, like the
telescoping legs of a tripod, a series of tapering
structures. Since it's quite far from one end to the
other, they can be opened out like an accordion;
but they can also be stacked inside one another
like Russian dolls, for the walls around time-
periods are extremely close to one another. The
people of other centuries hear our phonographs
blaring, and through the walls of time we see them
raising their hands towards the deliciously
prepared meal.

ELISABETH LENK

Introduction

by Margaret Atwood

Of all the seductive, sinister and transgressive women who have
haunted the Western imagination, none has a reputation more lurid
than Medea's. Judith, Salome, Jezebel, Delilah, Lady Macbeth—
these murdered or betrayed grown men, but Medea's crimes are yet
more chilling: credited with having slaughtered her younger brother,
she is also said to have sacrificed her own two children out of revenge for rejected love.

The Greek myth—so old it is spoken of as ancient by Homer—
has many variations, but it goes roughly as follows. Aeson, king of
Iolcus in Thessaly, had his throne usurped by his half brother Pelias.
Aeson's son Jason was saved, and sent away to be educated by the
centaur Cheiron. Grown to manhood, he arrived at the court of
Pelias to claim his birthright, but Pelias said he would surrender the
throne only on condition that Jason bring back the Golden Fleece

from Colchis—a demand which was thought to be the equivalent of a death sentence, as Colchis, situated at the extreme end of the Black Sea, was thought to be unreachable.

The Golden Fleece was the skin of the flying ram which had rescued Jason's ancestors, Phrixos and Helle, from threatened murder at the hands of their stepmother. Arrived safely at Colchis, Phrixos in gratitude sacrificed the ram and hung its fleece up in the temple of the war god Ares. Jason had either to refuse the quest and give up all hope of the throne, or accept it and endanger his life. He chose the latter course, and summoned fifty heroes from all over Greece to his aid. These were the Argonauts—named after their ship—who after many perils and adventures arrived at last at Colchis, a "barbarian" kingdom with strange customs—where, for instance, men's bodies were not buried, but suspended in sacks from trees. There Jason demanded the Golden Fleece as his by inheritance.

Aeëtes, King of Colchis, set more impossible conditions: Jason must harness two fire-breathing brazen-footed bulls, defeat the earth-born warriors that would spring up after he had sown a field with serpents' teeth, and slay the deadly dragon that guarded the Fleece. Jason was ready to admit defeat when he was seen by Princess Medea, daughter of Aeëtes, granddaughter of Helius the sun god, priestess of the Triple Goddess of the Underworld, and a powerful sorceress renowned for her ability to heal as well as to destroy. Overcome by love for Jason, she used her occult knowledge to help him surmount the various obstacles and to obtain the Fleece, in return for which Jason swore by all the gods to remain true to her forever. Together with the Argonauts, the two lovers set sail by night; but once the alarm was raised, King Aeëtes and the Colchians followed them.

Here traditions differ. Some say Jason killed Medea's younger brother Apsyrtus with a spear as he stood in a pursuing ship; others, that Medea herself murdered the boy, dismembered him, and scattered the pieces in the ocean. The grieving Aeëtes had to collect them and was thus delayed, and so the Argonauts escaped. In any case, the two needed to be purified for the death of Apsyrtus, and went to the island of the enchantress Circe, Medea's aunt and a daughter of Helius. After several more escapades—Medea, for instance, did away with the usurping King Pelias by tricking his own daughters into killing him, thus making Jason's own kingdom an even unhealthier place for him to be—the two, now lawfully man and wife, were welcomed at Corinth by its King, Creon.

It's at this point that the story turns from romantic adventure to tragedy. For Jason, forgetting both his debt of gratitude and his vows to all the gods, forsook his loyalty to Medea. Some say he was swayed by the insinuations of Creon—why live with such a dangerous woman, so much wiser and more powerful than yourself?—others, that he was overcome by a new love; others, that he was impelled by ambition; but in any case he decided to repudiate Medea, and to marry Creon's daughter Glauce, thus becoming the heir to Corinth. Medea herself was to be banished from the city.

Medea, torn by conflicting emotions—sorrow for lost love, wounded pride, rage, jealousy, hatred—concocted a horrible revenge. Pretending to accept Jason's decision and to wish for peace between them, she sent a bridal gift to Glauce—a beautiful but poisonous dress, which, when the rays of the sun hit it, burst into flame, whereupon Glauce in agony threw herself into a well. Some say that the people of Corinth then stoned Medea's children to death; others, that she herself killed them, either to save them from a worse fate or to pay Jason back for his treachery. She then disappeared from Corinth, some say in a chariot drawn by dragons. Jason himself, abandoned by the gods whom he had forsworn, became a wandering vagabond and was at last crushed by the prow of his own rotting ship.

This story has been retold time and again over the past two

and a half millennia. It has been used as the source for poems, plays, paintings, prose fiction, and operas, of which last there are twenty-four at least. Each artist has chosen among the variant traditions, and some have made their own changes and additions. For instance, we owe the slain children—two, not fourteen, as earlier versions had it—to the oddly sympathetic play by the Greek tragedian Euripides; and the many operas in which Medea sets fire to the temple of Hera and burns herself to death borrow this fiery finish from the seventeenth-century French dramatist Corneille. The poet Ovid is most interested in the eye-of-newt dimension, and spends much time on moonlit sorcery; the Roman dramatist Seneca goes in for unbridled rhetoric and gore. William Morris, in his narrative poem *The Life and Death of Jason,* gives us a blushing, trembling, Pre-Raphaelite maiden, reduced to a weepy pulp by Jason's infidelity, and a blonde into the bargain; Charles Kingsley, he of *Water Babies* fame, tries for a muscular-Christian interpretation—keep away from the bad women, lads, especially dark-haired witches! Each author has redone Medea in the light of his or her own age and its concerns; and so does Christa Wolf.

Her attack is head-on and original. Others before her have condemned Medea's main crimes—fratricide, infanticide, and the murder of the bride-elect Glauce by toxic frock—or viewed them as partially understandable under the circumstances, but Christa Wolf's Medea flatly denies that she committed any of these crimes at all. Drawing on the insights of modern anthropology, Wolf sets *Medea* in a period in which the old goddess-centered religions are being overwhelmed by new patriarchal god–ruled ones, in which kings are flouting the rights of queens, and in which former customs—including human sacrifice and the yearly dismemberment of the king in a fertility ritual—are falling into obsolescence, although they still have enough true believers to be resurrected by various rulers for their own purposes, most often the solidification of power. The murder and dismemberment of Apsyrtus, then, are seen to have a kinship with, for instance, the death of Orpheus, torn to pieces by Maenads at the Spring Festival; and Medea's betrayal of her father Aeëtes, and the aid she gives to Jason, are not ascribed, as usual, to an overwhelming passion caused by a shaft from naughty Cupid's golden bow, but to her secret knowledge of her father's role in the murder of his own son and dynastic rival.

In Wolf's version, Jason is beloved, true, but later: this Medea is no helpless slave of sexual passion. At first Jason is largely the means to an end—Medea's escape from blood-smeared Colchis in search of a higher and more humane civilization. Jason's betrayal of her is also Corinth's betrayal of her idealistic quest, and her contempt for his behavior is the contempt of the disillusioned nineteenth-century colonial arriving in Paris or London to find that the imperial promises of a nobler life ring hollow.

But *Medea* is neither an anthropological retelling of myth in the style of Mary Renault, nor a simpleminded story of men-versus-women, of a sensuous moon-and-earth religion versus a cold and abstract sky theology. It is a study of power, and of the operations of power, and of the behavior of human beings under pressure when power squeezes them tight.

Wolf begins her story in Corinth, at the moment when Medea has been rejected by Jason and the forces ranged against her are coming fully into play. Medea and the band of Colchians who have escaped with her are immigrants and refugees among the Corinthians. The Colchians have brown skin and woolly hair, in contrast to the pallid Corinthians. They keep to themselves in their own quarter, following their own customs and leading the marginal and often squalid life of exiles, and are viewed as aliens and therefore as ideal scapegoats for anything that might go wrong. Medea, as their princess and erstwhile leader, a healer and wise woman—one step away in reputation from sinister witch—is particularly exposed. Jason's position is ambiguous: a ruler in his own right, he cannot however claim his kingdom, and holds whatever power he possesses at the whim of King Creon, who is using Jason to further his own ambitions. Medea's star is falling, Jason's is rising, and the courtiers and hangers-on at the Palace—even Medea's friends and her former pupil—engage in a Machiavellian dance, as each one approaches and retreats. Shall they further their own careers by hastening her decline, shall they lend her a small and furtive helping hand, or shall they stand by and watch passively? Does Medea still have the power to retaliate, or has she been rendered harmless? Fear, admiration, envy, lust and hatred waltz hand-in-hand, for whatever else she is, Medea is not a nobody: beautiful, high-ranking, reckless, intelligent and skilled, she cannot be simply dismissed.

Medea herself is the wise child who knows too much and can't keep her mouth entirely shut about the Emperor's lack of clothing. One of the things she knows is the real manner of her brother Apsyrtus's death, which Creon is now trying to pin on her by means of a whispering campaign. Another thing she knows is the dirty little secret of Corinth itself. She's been down into the dark places, down into the cellar, and has discovered that Corinth, with its wealth and grandeur and snobbery, and its pretensions to a higher form of civilization, is no better than Colchis: deny and conceal the fact as it may, its power too is founded upon the sacrifice of children. Like many a civilization before and after it, Corinth rests on the oppression of the weak and the death of the innocent. So much knowledge is dangerous; but Creon and his toadies cannot confront Medea with what she knows without admitting that they know the same thing themselves, and the thing itself is unspeakable. Cat watches mouse, but which will turn out to be which?

Wolf's intention in this gripping retelling is signaled by her initial quotation from Elisabeth Lenk: ". . . the walls around time-periods are extremely close to one another. The people of other centuries hear our phonographs blaring, and through the walls of time we see them raising their hands towards the deliciously prepared meal." This tale is about Medea, yes; but it is also about us. Like J. M. Coetzee's extraordinary novel *Waiting for the Barbarians,* which is about an imagined empire but also about the collapse of apartheid in South Africa, and like Ryszard Kapuscinski's tour-de-force *The Emperor,* which is about the last days of Ethiopia's Haile Selassie but also about the corrupt communist regime in Poland, Wolf's *Medea* stirs up uneasy resonances. At one moment we're identifying the dark-skinned Colchians with, perhaps, the Turks in Germany, or those of African descent in Europe and North America, or the Jews; at another, we seem to be in the atmosphere of distrust and betrayal that characterized the collapse of the East German hegemony, when to back-stab first appeared to be the only defense against having the knife plunged swiftly into your own spine. Yet again, we're in the era of big business—our own time and place, here and now, when capitalist mini-kingdoms form and dissolve unseen within the walls erected around them by large corporations, when chieftains' heads roll bloodlessly, lopped off over lunch by faithless right-hand men, when pretexts abound and true texts get shredded, when spies are everywhere and even the watercoolers have ears.

Medea is no two-dimensional allegory. Like a tunnel full of mirrors, it both reflects and echoes. The question it asks the reader, through many voices and in many different ways, is: What would you be willing to believe, to accept, to conceal, to do, to save your own skin, or simply to stay close to power? Who would you be willing to sacrifice? Hard questions, but the posing of them is the troubling yet essential task of this tough, ingenious, brilliant and necessary book.

The Voices

MEDEA	Colchian. Daughter of Aeëtes, King of Colchis, and his wife, Eidyia. Sister of Chalciope and Apsyrtus
JASON	Argonaut, commander of the *Argo*
AGAMEDA	Colchian. Formerly Medea's pupil
AKAMAS	Corinthian. King Creon's First Astronomer
LEUKON	Corinthian. King Creon's Second Astronomer
GLAUCE	Corinthian. Daughter of King Creon and Queen Merope

Other Characters

CREON	King of Corinth
MEROPE	Queen of Corinth
IPHINOE	Their murdered daughter
TURON	Corinthian. Akamas's assistant
LYSSA	Colchian. Medea's foster sister and companion
ARINNA	Lyssa's daughter
CIRCE	Sorceress. Medea's mother's sister
PRESBON	Colchian. Organizer of the Corinthian Games
TELAMON	Jason's companion. Argonaut
PHRIXOS	Bringer of the Golden Fleece from Iolcus to Colchis
PELIAS	Jason's uncle, King of Iolcus
CHEIRON	Jason's tutor in the Thessalian mountains
MEIDOS, PHERES	Sons of Jason and Medea
OISTROS	Sculptor, Medea's lover
ARETHUSA	Cretan. Medea's friend
OLD MAN	Cretan. Arethusa's lover and friend

We pronounce a name, and—since the walls are porous—we step into her time, the wished-for meeting takes place, without hesitation she returns our gaze from the depths of the past. A child-murderess¿ For the first time, this doubt. A disdainful shrug; she turns away; she has no need of our doubt, of our endeavors to do her justice, she just goes. Ahead of us¿ Receding from us¿ These questions have lost their meaning on the way. We've summoned her to make this journey, she's coming toward us out of the depths of time, and we let ourselves fall back, back through ages that don't seem to speak to us so clearly as hers. At some point we must meet.

Do we let ourselves go back to the ancients, or do they catch up with us¿ No matter. An outstretched hand suffices. Lightly they cross over to us, our strange guests who are like ourselves. We hold the key that unlocks all epochs, sometimes we use it shamelessly, darting a hasty glimpse through the crack of the door, keen on quick, ready-made judgments; yet it should also be possible to get closer, a step at a time, awed by the taboo, unwilling without great need to wrest away a secret from the dead. Confessing our need—we should begin with that.

The millennia melt away under heavy pressure. So can the pressure be maintained¿ Idle question. Ill-considered questions trouble the uneasy shape that seeks to step out from the shadows of misjudgment. We must warn her. Nothing can refute our misjudgment, it forms a closed system. Or we must venture into the deepest core of our misjudgment—of her and of ourselves—simply walk in, with one another, behind one another, while the crash of the collapsing walls sounds in our ears. Next to us, or so we hope, is the shape with the magical name, in whom the epochs meet—a painful process—and in whom our time meets us. The wild woman.

Now we hear Voices.

One

Medea

Everything that I have done thus far
I call a work of charity . . .
Now I am Medea;
My nature has grown through
    suffering.

SENECA, *Medea*

*E*ven dead gods reign. Even the hapless fear for their happiness. The language of dreams. The language of the past. Help me up, up out of this shaft, away from this clanging in my head, why do I hear the clash of weapons, does that mean they're fighting, who's fighting, Mother, my Colchians, am I hearing their war games in our inner courtyard, or where am I, because the clashing keeps getting louder. Thirsty. I must wake up. I must open my eyes. The pitcher next to the bed. Cool water doesn't just quench my thirst, it stills the noise in my brain too. But I know about that. You sat there next to me, Mother, and if I turned my head like this I could see out the window, as I can here, where am I? There wasn't any fig tree there, that's where my favorite walnut tree was. Did you know that one could yearn for a tree, Mother? I was a child, nearly a child, I'd bled for the first time, but I wasn't sick on that account, and it wasn't on that account that you sat by me and made the time pass, changing the herb poultices on my chest and forehead, holding my hands up in front of my eyes and showing me the lines in my palms, first the left one, then the right, how different from one another. You taught me to read them. I've often tried to ignore their messages; I've clenched my hands into fists, wrung them, laid them on wounds, raised them to the goddess, carried water from the spring, woven linen with our patterns; I've buried my hands in the warm hair of children. Once, Mother, in another time, I took your head in my hands as I bade you farewell, its shape is still impressed on my palms—hands can remember too. These hands have palpated every part of Jason's body, as recently as last night, but now it's morning, and what a day.

Easy. Take it easy, one step at a time. Concentrate. Where are you? I'm in Corinth. The fig tree in front of the window opening in this clay hut was a solace to me when they expelled me from King Creon's palace. Why? That comes later. Is the banquet over, or must I still attend it? After all, I promised Jason. You can't let me down now, Medea, a lot depends on this banquet. Not for me, I told him, as you well know; still and all, if that's what you want, I'll come, I said, but this is the last time. Long ago you traced that tiny line in my left palm with your fingernail and told me what it would mean if it should ever cross the life line, you knew me very well, Mother, are you still alive?

Look here. See, that tiny line is deeper now, and it crosses the other one. Beware, you told me, arrogance will turn your insides cold. Maybe so, but pain, Mother, pain leaves an awful trail behind too. I don't have to tell *you* that. It was pitch-dark when we boarded the *Argo,* but I still saw your eyes, I couldn't forget them, and their gaze burned into my brain a word I'd never known before: guilt.

Now I hear that clashing again, it must be the fever, yet it seems to me I was sitting at that table, not exactly by Jason's side, was that yesterday? Stay here, Mother, why am I so tired? I just want to sleep a little while longer, I'll get up soon, I'll put on that white dress I wove and sewed myself, just the way you taught me, and then we'll walk together again through the corridors of our palace, and I'll be happy, as when I was a child and you took me by the hand and led me to the fountain in the courtyard—you know, I've never come across a lovelier fountain anywhere—and one of the women draws up the wooden bucket for us, and I ladle out the spring water and drink and drink and grow healthy again.

So this is how it is: either I'm out of my mind, or their city is founded on a crime. No, believe me, I'm quite clear on this point, what I say or think about it is quite clear to me, for I've found the proof, yes, I've touched it with my own hands. Oh, it's not arrogance that threatens to undo me now. The woman—I simply followed her. Perhaps I just wanted to teach Jason a lesson, since he'd stood by and let them seat me at the end of the table among the servants, that's it, I didn't dream that, that was yesterday. At least they're the highest-ranking servants, he said pathetically, don't cause a scandal, Medea, please, not today, you know what's at stake, the King can't lose face in front of all his foreign guests. Ah, Jason, save your breath. He still hasn't understood that King Creon can't grieve me anymore, but that's not what I'm talking about, I have to clear my head. I have to promise myself never to speak about my discovery to a living soul. The best thing would be to do what Chalciope and I used to do with secrets when we were children, do you know what that was, Mother? We'd wrap our secret up tight in a leaf and eat it up while staring into one another's eyes. Our childhood—or rather everything in Colchis—was full of dark secrets, and when I arrived here, a refugee in King Creon's gleaming city-state of Corinth, I had an envious thought: these people have no secrets. And that's what they think too, that's what makes them so convincing; with every look, with every one of their measured movements, they're drumming it into you: Here's one place in the world where a person can be happy. It was only later that I realized how much they hold it against you if you express doubts about their happiness. But that's not what I'm talking about either, what's the matter with my head? It's buzzing with a whole swarm of thoughts, why is it so hard for me to reach into the swarm and snatch out the one thought I need?

I had the good fortune to be seated at the King's table between my friend Leukon, Creon's Second Astronomer, and Telamon. You know him too, Mother, he was the Argonaut who came to the palace with Jason after they landed on the Colchian coast. So I knew I wouldn't be bored at the banquet. Leukon's a clever man, I love to talk with him, there's a sympathy between us; and Telamon, though perhaps a bit uncouth, has been devoted to me since that first afternoon in Colchis, so many years ago that I can hardly count them. In my presence he always tries to be especially witty, also especially obscene, we all had to laugh. Resolved to punish the King from my lowly place, I acted the part of a princess—which is, after all, what I am, right, Mother? A great Queen's daughter. It wasn't hard for me to attract notice and demand respect, even from the foreign emissaries, the Libyans and the Mediterranean islanders. Telamon played along; we had poor Jason in a tight spot, torn between jealousy and his eagerness to please a King we're all, of course, dependent on. He lifted a surreptitious glass to me, cautioning me with stern looks not to let my exuberance go too far, but whenever the King launched into one of his tirades Jason had to hang on his lips. We were having a merry time at our end of the table, now everything's coming back to me again. How the two men at my sides began to quarrel over me, how Leukon, tall, thin, a bit awkward, with his oval-shaped skull that understands jokes but can't make any, started to extol my abilities as a healer to Telamon, a giant with curly blond hair, and how thereupon Telamon went into loud raptures over my physical attributes, my brown skin, he said, for example, my woolly hair that all we Colchians have, that's what conquered Jason right away, and him besides, but what was he compared to Jason, and then he became sentimental, strong men do that so easily, my burning eyes, he said. Yes, you *do* know him, Mother, whenever I see him I remember how you put your hand to your mouth as though in fright and yelled out Aiee! when he appeared in our doorway. It was a cry of appreciation, if I'm not mistaken, and I remember how your eyes sparkled, and how I noticed that you were by no means an old woman yet, and then against my will my sour-faced, suspicious father crossed my mind. Ah, Mother. I'm not a young woman anymore, but according to the Corinthians I'm still wild, as far as they're concerned a woman is wild if she has a mind of her own. The Corinthian women seem like thoroughly tamed house pets to me, they stare at me as though I'm some strange apparition, and we three merrymakers at the end of the table drew all eyes upon us, all the courtiers' envious, indignant eyes, and also poor Jason's pleading ones—well, yes.

Why did I follow that woman, the Queen, when I'd barely caught a glimpse of her during all my years in Corinth? Wrapped up in a thick cocoon of bloodcurdling rumors, securely hidden behind her unapproachability, she passes her days and her nights in the remotest, oldest wing of the palace, inside thick-walled rooms said to resemble dimly lit caves, fitter for a prisoner than a sovereign, served and guarded by two peculiarly rugged females who, however, are supposed to be quite devoted to her in their way. I don't believe she knows my name, and I had never wasted a thought on the unhappy Queen of a country that has always seemed alien to me and will stay that way forever. How my head aches, Mother, something inside me balks at climbing down into those caves again, into the Underworld, into Hades—where for ages people have died and been born again, where living beings are baked fresh from the humus of the dead—and so back to the mothers, back to the goddess of death. But what can forward and back mean there? My fever's mounting—I had to do it. The first time I saw this woman at Creon's side, Mother, it was with that second sight that you recognized in me. I struggled with all my might against becoming the pupil of that young priest, I preferred getting sick. Now I remember; it was during that same sickness that you showed me the lines in my palms, and later that priest committed some dreadful crimes, he wasn't a normal person, and that's when you said, the child has second sight. I've almost lost it here, sometimes I think the Corinthians' morbid fear of what they call my magical powers has robbed me of my gift. And so I was shocked when I saw Queen Merope. She was sitting beside King Creon without a word, she seemed to hate him and he seemed to fear her—anyone with eyes in his head could have seen that. I mean something else. I mean that suddenly it became completely quiet. That I had that flickering in front of my eyes that comes before second sight. That in the vast banquet hall this woman and I were alone. I saw her there, her aura almost completely darkened by inconsolable grief, so much so that I was horror-stricken and I had to follow her when she stood up stiffly in her gold-embroidered formal dress as soon as the meal was over and left the room without a word of explanation, without so much as a good night for the foreign merchants and emissaries, thus forcing the King to cover up her impertinence by talking fast and laughing loudly. His defeat rejoiced my heart. He must have forced this woman to present her ravaged face to all those vain, prying people just as Jason had brought me to the point of performing a little comedy for them. Now I'd had enough. Both of us left for the same reason: pride. You once told me, and I've never forgotten it, that anyone who wanted to kill me would have to deal more blows to my pride than to anything else. Nothing has changed in that regard, nor will it, and it would be a good thing for my poor Jason to grasp this fact before too long.

I followed the woman. That passage, the one that leads to the banquet hall—how often have I walked along it at Jason's side, the respected wife of the royal nephew and guest-friend, in times that seemed happy to me. How could I have deceived myself so thoroughly? But nothing is so deceptive as happiness, and there's no place that clouds clarity of perception so much as a place in the retinue of a King. It looked as though the earth had swallowed up Merope, there had to be some sort of hatch or opening somewhere, I searched around and found it hidden behind a pile of pelts. I took one of the burning torches from its holder and slipped into the passageway, which soon became so low that I had to walk stooped over, or did I dream that, the gloomy, vaulted cellarage, the King's bright glorious palace as its own counterimage in the depths of the earth, built into the darkness. The stone stairs, down one flight after another, I must have dreamed that; but the cold, surely that was no dream, I'm still shivering, nor the sharp-edged stones that tore my skin, why else would my arms be so covered with crusted scratches? And then at the bottom, at the deepest level, in that cellar where even in this dry country there were pools of water, the entrance to a labyrinth of caves, two steps and then down on my belly, crawling forward, protecting the torch that was only flickering now, not thinking anymore about Merope, who might or might not be ahead of me, not thinking about anything or anyone anymore, just knowing I must go on, on and on; when the passage finally broadened into a cave, it was familiar to me from my dreams—if not, how did I know that the way forked there, how did I know that I had to keep to my left and that soon my torch would go out? It went out. At that point the passage was so narrow that I would have had to crawl backward to get out, therefore I had to keep going, knowing full well it could mean my undoing—one's always hearing about someone who got lost while exploring underground caves and died inside them. Do I want to die, the question crossed my mind, I set my teeth and kept on crawling, then I licked some moisture seeping from the walls, tasteless dampness, then I sensed that the composition of the air was changing, and then my hair stood up even before I heard the sound. Then I heard the sound. It lasted longer than a person has breath, a barely audible but penetrating whining. It could just as well have been an animal, but it was no animal.

It was the woman. It was Merope. I wanted to go back, all the way back, and I pushed myself forward inch by inch. All at once, the sound stopped; the hammer in my chest drowned out any other noise, it hasn't stopped, it's hammering all the way up to my temples. Then, when my eyes had glimpsed the right direction in the darkness, I saw the Queen, sitting in the dim light of her little oil lamp, braced straight and still against the rocky cave wall, her eyes unwaveringly fixed on a point across from her. In this icy cold I was drenched with sweat, I stank of horror, such a thing had never happened to me. Something stirred in me that I had kept locked up and almost forgotten, something came alive in that corpses' crypt. This wasn't a game anymore. That whole production at the King's table, how vain that had been, how vain and affected my own behavior. But I've known one thing for a long time: there's a role in the big machine even for someone who makes fun of it. I wasn't going in for that sort of thing very much anymore, it's true, yet I must admit that I let a trace of coquetry spur me on at the King's banquet, instead of Merope's total, uncompromising refusal, and now she'd led me here, to the bottom of the Underworld, where my horror was suddenly replaced by panic, because there was something uncannily silent creeping in there, something I must hide from, but there weren't any cracks or fissures in the rock. Whatever was slithering this way had learned to move soundlessly, without causing so much as a current of air, even better than I can do it. For you taught me how to move like that at a very early age, Mother, showed me movement made up of tiny non-movements, and I learned how to melt into walls too—

I'd need that in my father's palace, you said, before I understood why—as well as the breathing that holds back every breath that would otherwise escape from a person's body; all I'd learned was still there, it took over the commands and stopped me from shivering out loud at the sight of the creature, the shadow of a shadow, that propelled itself to the woman's side, whispered a word to her, and took the dimming lamp out of her hand. Whereupon the Queen allowed herself to be led away by this female, as I now perceived her to be, and as the cave narrowed they both had to go down on their knees, a movement that I involuntarily imitated. I knelt down, either out of weakness or out of gratitude to a god who had extricated me from yet another predicament. Or out of mortal fear.

I waited until the women were out of earshot, and then I began to feel my way along the walls of the cave. I had to know this Queen's secret. In complete darkness my fingertips found what I suppose they were looking for: scratches in the stone not put there by nature, surfaces scraped with tools familiar to me from Colchis, lines that I could follow until they formed signs and figures which, as I knew, people here in Corinth carved in the cave graves of the eminent dead. This jibed with the suspicion I wouldn't yet have been able to express. At the spot where Merope had sat, I went down on all fours and crawled across to the wall the Queen had stared at, felt with reluctant fingers for the deep niche carved into the rock, found what I had feared to find, and uttered a cry that echoed in the maze of caves. Then I retraced my steps. I had learned what I wanted to know, I promised myself to forget it as soon as possible, and since then I can think of nothing but that meager, childish skull, those fine-boned shoulder blades, that brittle spinal column. Ah me.

The city is founded on a monstrous deed.

Whoever gives away this secret is lost. I needed the shock to make my way back. Not back to the King's table and the disdainful scowls of the company, surely not. But where to go? Not even you would be able to advise me this time, Mother, I can consult the lines in my palms as much as I want, and very distinct lines they are, but what does that mean here and now? However wretched it makes me feel, this illness means to give me a breathing space. I can fathom the hidden significance of illness, but I know how to use it better for healing others than for healing myself. Half intentionally, I abandon myself to the fever that's rising in me, washing me away on a fiery wave, and bringing me images, shreds of images, faces.

Jason. Did I betray myself to him? No. There was a moment, a fleeting, seductive moment, but I kept quiet. Yes I did, I kept quiet. Jason was waiting for me, I hadn't reckoned on that, I still don't know him completely, I've avoided knowing him completely be- cause it wasn't important to me anymore—a convenient but danger- ous omission. Instead of sparing no effort to anticipate his every impulse, I afforded myself the luxury of indifference; otherwise I would have realized that the mixture of triumph and humiliation he'd experienced at the King's banquet table would arouse his desire to such a point that only I could satisfy it, not any of the palace girls, ready and willing though they are.

Exhausted and dirty, I dragged myself home, home to the clay hovel stuck on the palace wall like a bird's nest and vaulted over by the fig tree whose bright leaves I can see from my bed. Lyssa's look warned me, the way her lips moved was a hint as to who was waiting for me behind the curtained doorway of the next room. I had just time enough to rinse my face and hands and throw on a clean nightgown in place of my torn and filthy dress before Jason called for me. The best way to deceive people is to make a show of perfectly ordinary behavior, so as usual I had to shove Jason's things, which he as usual had simply let fall, out of the way, and in so doing stretch out my foot from under the long, loose gown with that graceful, conscious movement, aware that Jason likes women's feet and that no woman has feet more beautiful than mine. He said so again, and to gain time I asked him if he remembered when he'd taken my feet in his hands for the first time, and he answered, with great assurance, Stupid question. Come here. That's the way the man speaks to me now, and it doesn't even matter to me anymore that he mixes me up with his other women. I told him he had to answer me first. There are certain things that a man just doesn't forget, he said, and immediately gave me an example of his capacity for forgetting.

It was in Colchis, he said, we were sitting by that stockade that fences off the inner palace courtyard from the other ones, it was night and a full moon, I remember that quite clearly. You were wearing a gown like this one, he said, I'd never seen such a weave, on the other side of the fence the watchmen were bawling out those horrible songs of yours that put trouble in a man's soul. When he said this I remembered how those long-drawn-out, melancholy songs our young soldiers sing used to seize my heart too, not for the same reasons. You promised, Jason said, to help me get that god-damned Fleece, the sole purpose of our long journey, and I—well yes, if you must know—I took your foot in my hands. Now come.

I was astonished, but at myself. He can still hurt me, Mother, that has to stop. Besides, it should have been obvious to me that he, too, could think of only one reason why I helped him against my own father: I must have been helplessly in thrall to him, Jason. They all think that, all the Corinthians, in any case—as far as they're concerned, a woman's love for a man explains and excuses every-thing. But our Colchians, too, the ones who left with me, thought Jason and I were lovers from the beginning. The notion that I couldn't have slept in my father's house with a man who was de-ceiving him won't penetrate their thick skulls. Deceiving him with my help, Mother, yes, yes indeed, that's what was so cruel about the position I was in, that's what was tearing me apart, I couldn't make a move that wasn't false, I couldn't do anything that didn't betray something dear to me. I know what the Colchians must have called me after I fled, Father surely saw to that: Traitress. The word still stings me. It stung me that night on the *Argo,* one of the first nights after our flight, the Colchian fleet had broken off its pursuit, I was at the side of the ship, perched on a coil of rope, there was a new moon and an enormous, starry sky. Don't you remember, I could have asked Jason, the shooting stars were falling into the sea as though strewn by someone's hand, the waters were calm, the waves were washing quietly against the sides of the ship, the Argonauts on rowing duty were rowing along rhythmically, quietly, the ship was gently rocking, the night was mild. When you came, Jason, I could have told him, you were a dark shadow against the starry sky; you were at your best, you said the right thing in the right way, you soothed my grief, which you knew nothing of and which I considered beyond remedy. As if to warm them, you took my feet in your hands.

Nonsense, Jason would have said, so I kept quiet. He said, Let's not fight, Medea. Not tonight. Come. In his voice, once again, was the signal that something in me answers. Once again I abandoned myself to him, not just my foot but every part of my body, he responds to it like no other man. Used to respond to it is perhaps more accurate. Jason? Long silence. I'd seen him like this before. Now he'd have to find someone to blame. This happens, he said accusingly, because you're deceiving me. If not, where did you disappear to so soon after the banquet, who were you having fun with? I couldn't answer his questions, and that made him angry. In the past, he said, you wouldn't have acted like this. In the past, you gave me strength, all the strength I needed. What he said was true. I got up and rinsed my hands and face with the water I'd drawn from the spring in the morning. In the past, I said to Jason, in the past you believed in me. And in yourself.

You always have a clever answer, Jason said, you always know better, when will you admit that your time has passed? Now, I said, surprised as I was, now I admit it, but what good does it do you? Then he pressed his head between his hands and gave such a groan as I'd never heard from him before. Don't think, he said, just don't think it makes me feel better when you don't know what to do either. That was a confession I wouldn't have expected from him. I sat down next to him on the bed, tugged his hands away from his temples, stroked his forehead, his cheeks, his shoulders, the vulnerable hollow in his collarbone. Come, he said, pleading, and I lay down beside him, I know his body, know how to ignite his desire, behind his closed eyelids he abandoned himself to the fantasies he never let me share. Yes, yes, yes, Medea, that's the way. I wished him success, he succeeded, fell on me with all his weight, buried his face between my breasts, and wept for a long time. I had never seen him cry. Then he stood up, plunged his face into the water basin on the chest, shook his head like an ox that's just been struck between the eyes, and left without turning to me again.

I'll have to pay for that. In Corinth, if a woman sees a man's weakness, she always has to pay.

And at home? In Colchis? Am I fooling myself if I privately insist that things were different there? It's odd, lately, how I practice calling up the memory of Colchis and filling it with colors, as if I simply refused to watch Colchis fading in me. Or as if I needed it, I don't yet know why.

I went to Lyssa's room, she was still awake. Next door, through the curtain, I heard the children's breathing. I was hoping Lyssa would ask me where I'd been, but she never asks. Among all living things, she's the one from whom I've never been separated for a single day, she, who was born the same day I was, whose mother was my wet nurse, she, who was the wet nurse of my children. She, who's seen everything with me and probably understood everything—or was that an illusion too, when I considered it normal for her to empathize with all my feelings and expected her to perceive them, often before I did and even when I denied them to her face? Lyssa, whom I sometimes pull down next to me on the bed for an intimate chat, and whom I sometimes wish away at the edge of the world. But the edge of the world is Colchis. Our Colchis on the southern slopes of the wild Caucasus Mountains, whose stark outline is inscribed in every one of us—we know this about one another, but we never speak of it, speaking increases homesickness until it can't be borne. But I knew that, I knew I'd never stop pining for Colchis. Still, what can that mean, "knew"? This ache that never goes away, that's always gnawing, you can't know it in advance, we Colchians read it in one another's eyes when we gather to sing our songs and tell our young folk the tales of our gods and our forefathers—which many of them don't want to hear anymore, because they think it's important to act like real Corinthians. Sometimes I, too, avoid those gatherings, and it strikes me that they're inviting me less and less often. Ah, my beloved Colchians, they understand how to hurt me too. And lately Lyssa has learned the trick as well.

Of course she had stayed awake, as she always does when I may need her, but unlike the other times, she refused to give me her complicitous smile. I wouldn't beg for this favor, I pretended to notice nothing and began, there in the middle of the night, a discussion about whether the men in Colchis were different from the ones in Corinth. She joined in the game austerely; as far as she recalled, the men in Colchis gave vent to their feelings, she said, for example after her brother's accident her father had wept publicly and bitterly, had howled and moaned, while at a Corinthian funeral you never see a man weeping—the women must take care of that for the men. Then she grew silent. I knew what she was thinking about. I've never seen a man weep as that young Colchian did, the one Lyssa loved with such devotion, but whom she left behind to follow me onto the *Argo* for an uncertain journey. She gave birth to her daughter, Arinna, during the voyage, and thereafter there has been no man in Lyssa's life, and I can't help asking myself what price Lyssa has paid, and the other Colchians, and all of us, because I didn't want to live in Colchis anymore and they followed me, blinded by my good repute among them. That's the way I must look at it today.

Jason? Ah, Jason. I let them keep believing he was the man I'd follow to the ends of the earth, and I can't blame them for taking our separation as a serious personal offense. Worse: as proof that our flight was in vain. While I, I thought as I lay on Lyssa's bed, I touched that proof today with my own hands, a child's skeleton hidden away from all the world in a cave. Then Lyssa laid her hand on my neck. We still make the old gestures, but they no longer have the same meaning. We can soothe one another. We can't put anything right. That's not part of the arrangement, Mother, I'm beginning to understand.

What did I want to put right, or put back together, if the best course of action I could think of was to go with Jason? When I confided my intentions first to you, Mother, and then to Lyssa, both of you listened to me in silence, not even asking me my reasons, until finally Lyssa declared she'd come with me. It was only years later that I decided to ask her what was going on during those last days and nights in Colchis, for it was Lyssa who collected the little band of Colchians who were willing to join us. She couldn't afford a single miscalculation, every one of them had to be reliable, any thoughtless or treacherous word about our plan would have meant catastrophe. She understood our countrymen thoroughly—she'd observed them carefully for a long time—and she knew which of them found the situation at home as unbearable as I did. They didn't go along with us because of me, or not only because of me, Lyssa has often assured me of that, whenever my Colchians, disappointed by the lands to which I, a fugitive myself, have led them, begin to blame me for the loss of their homeland, which shines for them, belatedly, in all its pristine brilliance. How I understand them. How furious they often make me.

It wasn't long before differing and even contradictory stories began to circulate about the circumstances of our sailing from Colchis. What's certain is this: I went to Lyssa's bed and shook her awake—Come on, Lyssa, are you coming?—and she got up, grabbed the bundle she'd already packed, and slunk with me out of the palace and down to the shore, where the *Argo* lay waiting on a calm sea and in almost total darkness, and with it two other ships that belonged to the Colchian fleet, escape ships, to which men wading in the shallow waters were carrying the women and children who were coming with us. Early in the crossing some of these men began to exaggerate the depth of the water and, especially, to go on about how fraught with peril our departure had been, about swells and rough seas, and about their own courage and good judgment, by virtue of which all the women and children had made it safely on board. If our situation worsens, their legend-spinning will get completely out of hand, and objections based on facts will be futile. That is, if there still are such things as facts, after all these years. And if homesickness and humiliation and disappointment and poverty haven't worn them down to a thin, brittle shell that anyone who really wants to can destroy. Who will want to do that? Presbon?

Presbon, with his insatiable egoism—that could be. He was the only one of the emigrants whom Lyssa herself hadn't briefed, to this day she reproaches herself for having tolerated his coming. He seized the opportunity to turn his back on Colchis and offer his immense talent for self-display elsewhere, here in glittering Corinth, for example, where he's made himself indispensable to the production of the great temple festival plays. He knows how to set their complicated machinery in motion better than anyone, and his inspired performances of the great roles are such highlights that King Creon is moved to gratitude. No Colchian has been so highly honored as he, Presbon, the son of a maid and a palace guard officer in Colchis, who during our early days here in Corinth didn't consider himself too good to pick up rubbish from the grass after big holiday festivities. How much effort he had to make to get himself noticed. How he suffered from humiliation. How he hates everyone who saw him in his disgrace and mocked the contortions he put himself through in order to climb higher. How he hates me, because I wasn't capable of recognizing his true worth. Nothing fails to have consequences, Mother, you were right about that.

Was it Lyssa who told you what time we were to set sail? You guessed it yourself, more likely. No one studied as attentively as you did the events brought on by the appearance of those foreigners in Colchis.

Everything looked promising at first. Our Colchians weren't unsympathetic to them, to Jason with his panther skin and his rather unkempt band of Argonauts, who weren't so much brutish as awkward, ready to help when help was wanted, and curious. And it was actually flattering that the goal of their perilous sea voyage was none other than our Colchis, a land like others on the Black Sea coast. In any case, these mariners had dropped anchor in the mouth of our river Phasis, and there was no reason not to treat them with the courtesy due to guests. Besides, shortly after their arrival King Aeëtes, my father, received Jason and Telamon and invited all fifty Argonauts to the palace the following evening for a banquet which cost a quantity of sheep their lives and ended in high spirits and oaths of friendship.

Naturally there were many who later claimed to have smelled disaster, but what could have been sinister about such a banquet, the palace resounded with the noise of feasting and the blare of ram's-horn trumpets, for the wine we grow on the southern slopes of the mountains found great favor with our guests.

No. I was the only one with a premonition of evil, because I knew how suspiciously Father regarded these guests. The only one except for you, Mother. You didn't need any new reasons for gloomy premonitions. You knew the King. I had to deal with the father inside of me: You shall not betray me, my daughter. I knew that Jason wanted the Fleece. I knew that the King didn't want to give it to him. I didn't ask why not. My duty was to help Father render this man harmless, no matter what the price. I saw how high he set the price—too high for us all. The only choice left me was to betray him.

Did I have no other choice? How the years have washed away the reasons I used to be so sure of. Again and again I call to mind the sequence of those events—I've kept it locked up in my memory as a protective wall against the doubts that now, so late, are flooding through my defenses. A single word opened the breach: futility. Ever since I touched that child's little bones, my hands remember those other little bones, the ones that I—loudly weeping, I still remember that—threw from my fleeing ship to the King, who was pursuing us. Then he broke off the chase. After that, the Argonauts were afraid of me. Even Jason, whom I looked upon with different eyes after I saw the way he commanded his ship. He had poked around Colchis like a blind man, understood nothing, and put himself completely in my hands; but when he stepped aboard his ship, with the Fleece laid across his shoulders, he became another man. He lost all trace of awkwardness, he stiffened his spine, there was nothing unmanly in his concern for the fate of his crew, the prudent way he handled the Colchians' embarkation impressed me. Then I heard, for the first time, the word "refugee." To the Argonauts, we were refugees; I felt a pain in my heart. I gave up certain sensitivities around that time.

But that's not the point now. I believe it's my weakness, Mother, my momentary weakness, that's putting me at the mercy of these thoughts today. When you were standing on the shore to bid me farewell, you led me to believe that you approved of what I was doing. I had no choice. There wasn't much to say. Don't become like me, you said, then you pulled me against you with a strength I hadn't felt in you for a long time, turned away, and went up the embankment toward the palace, where the farewell drink I'd mixed for the King and his servants before they responded to Jason's departing toast had left them sleeping sound and deep. Jason himself had to remain alert and sober in order to find his way back to the sacred grove of Ares, which I had shown him by daylight, then to creep past the guards, who were also, thanks to me, sound asleep, and finally to perform—with my help—that feat for which he had come all the way to Colchis, at the eastern edge of his world: to take down from the oak sacred to the war god the ram's fleece that his uncle Phrixos, fleeing for his life, had brought there many years ago, and that his relatives were now demanding back. A sort of test of courage, or so I considered it at the time, unfamiliar as I was with poor Jason's tangled family history. It was only later, when they had looked at the thing more closely, that the *Argo*'s crewmen decided to call it the Golden Fleece, but what did the Fleece mean to me? Like the fleece of many a ram in Colchis, that ram's skin had been used for gathering gold, that is, one spring it was laid in the bed of one of the mountain torrents that rush down to the valley, and there it collected the gold dust that was being washed out of the mountain's innards. The Argonauts questioned me very closely about this method, which seemed quite ordinary to me but sent them into flurries of excitement. There was gold in Colchis! Real gold! Why hadn't I told them about this before? Think how much more profitable their enterprise might have been!

I didn't understand them until I came to Corinth. Corinth is obsessed with gold. Can you imagine, Mother, they don't just make cult objects and jewelry out of gold, but common things for everyday use, plates, bowls, vases, even sculptures, and they sell these things at exorbitant prices round about their Mediterranean Sea; and they're always more than ready to barter grain, cattle, horses, or weapons for unworked gold, for simple ingots. What we found most disconcerting was this: the worth of a Corinthian citizen is measured by the quantity of gold in his possession, and the contributions he must make to the palace are calculated accordingly. Entire armies of clerks are employed in making these calculations—Corinth is proud of her specialists in this field—and Akamas, the chief astronomer and the King's First Minister, to whom I once mentioned my astonishment over the multitude of these useless but arrogant scribes and reckoners, lectured me about their eminent usefulness in dividing the Corinthian people into different classes, which is the first means of making a country governable. But why gold, of all things, I asked. Surely you must know, he replied, that it's our wishes, our desires, that make one thing valuable and another one worthless. The father of our King Creon was a clever man. He made gold much sought-after in Corinth by means of a single prohibition: he proclaimed a law forbidding his subjects to wear gold jewelry unless their contributions to the palace reached a certain level. You, too, are a clever man, Akamas, I said to him. Your kind of cleverness didn't exist in Colchis. That's because it's not required in your country, he said, smiling again in the way that used to wound me in the early days. And he was probably right.

But where am I wandering off to? I must finally get up. If I'm seeing right, Mother, the rays of the sun are already falling onto the fig tree from directly overhead, can it be possible I've lain about dozing the entire morning, that's never happened before. It's because of the caves, I can't climb out of them, someone should help me, Lyssa should come, the children. There, someone's feeling my forehead, a voice says, You're sick, Medea.

Is that you, Lyssa.

Two

Jason

Mighty is the longing of man
to be remembered
and to make himself an immortal
name forever.

PLATO, *Symposium*

That woman will do me in. As if I haven't always known it. I said quite frankly to Akamas, Medea will do me in. He neither contradicted nor agreed with me, because that's his goddamned style. Always that cunning smile, always that knowing look in his eyes, always that glib talk designed to persuade me that no one can harm me so easily anymore. Whatever that's supposed to mean this time. No doubt he's got special insight, our worthy First Astronomer. Are you mocking me, Akamas, I yelled at him. He just looked distressed and shook his head, that great hollow-cheeked head of his on that strangely lopsided body where no joint matches any other. What efforts he makes to appear imposing, is the way Medea put it after meeting him for the first time, from the very beginning they've had uneasy relations, she just wouldn't meet him halfway. If you ask me, something nasty's going to happen.

Now he's her enemy. I don't know why, something must have escaped me, as so much escapes me in the confusion of this royal household, I have a hard time fitting in with their ways. My *Argo* dropped anchor in so many ports, in so many countries, I've looked into so many different human faces. Now that my ship's docked and my company's dispersed, this small spot is all I've got left, here is where I've got to make my way, and Medea's got to make her way here too, damn it all. As if that's so hard to grasp. She must have got on old Akamas's nerves, otherwise he wouldn't now be digging up that stale old story—still unproven to boot—and spreading it around. And so I had to stand before the Council of Elders like the ultimate dimwit and answer questions about the charge that Medea, back then, killed her brother. I felt as though I'd taken one to the head, I could only raise up my hands and protest, But that's completely out of the question. So, they said, you're certain that her accusers are lying?

What was I up against, what had she got me mixed up in this time? They wanted certainties? What can the likes of us be certain of when it comes to women? The elders nodded their heads in agreement. Apparently it's not me they've got it in for. But her. And she's my wife.

What *can* the likes of us be certain of, when these women are in agreement to let a man grope in the dark. And I mean that literally. It was indeed pitch-dark when Medea appeared at the landing place, carrying that hide bundle in her arms, her only baggage, she cradled that bundle almost like a newborn child. Up until the last moment I'd doubted that she would come. After all, I'd seen how she walked around her city, with her head up. How the people would gather around her, greet her. How she spoke with them. She knew every-one, a surge of expectation bore her along.

I saw her in her palace courtyard, drinking from the fountain, which is itself an amazing and marvelous thing. Water, milk, wine, and oil flow from its four spouts, which are set up exactly according to the four points of the compass. That's how I saw her for the first time: bent over the fountain, scooping out water with her hands and drinking it in thirsty delight. I was there with shaggy Telamon, who is perhaps not the cleverest but one of the merriest, most even-tempered of my Argonauts, and faithfully devoted to me. That's the reason he's still hanging around here, staying close to me, even now. It was in the middle of the afternoon, in the sweltering heat, which was taking its toll on us since we were used to cooling sea breezes, and we only a few hours in this country on which we'd focused all our thoughts and all our energies for so many weeks. What had it cost us to fight our way through to this place, on the edge of the world, we'd lost so many comrades, how often was the urge to turn around overpowering, and only the thought of shaming ourselves in one another's eyes and before those who would give us a spiteful welcome home kept us on our course. And then this wonderland, Colchis, was spread out before us—the land, it seemed to us, where our destiny would be decided.

Now, everybody knows that a period of slackness often follows intense effort. And so it happened with us, our jubilation at finally finding the main channel of their river Phasis and anchoring successfully in one of its natural backwaters was followed by a change in the general mood. So this was the land we'd so longed to reach. The river, its banks, the surrounding countryside—a hilly landscape thinly covered with mixed woodland—seemed mighty ordinary to us, we'd seen more impressive sights along the way. Naturally everyone refrained from saying a word about it, but I could read my men's disappointment in their eyes. And yet those who stayed behind on the *Argo* couldn't know what lay ahead of us when we, Telamon and I, set out to seek King Aeëtes's palace and present our demand to this unknown King.

My future fame was secured from the moment when I, first of all my companions, set foot on this easternmost and most alien coast; the thought gave me strength. We, who were advancing into a barbarian country, expected to encounter barbarian customs and steeled ourselves by calling in our hearts to our gods. But I can still feel today the shudder that seized me when we'd passed through the low shrubbery on the riverbank and found ourselves in a grove of regularly planted trees, which bore the most appalling fruit: cowskin, sheepskin, goatskin bags, and inside them, visible through rips and holes, were human bones, human mummies were hanging there, swaying in the gentle breeze, a horror for any civilized person, who shuts up his dead in the earth or in rock tombs. Horror penetrated our very limbs. We had to go on.

Then again the woman, the one who came up to us in Aeëtes's vine-covered court, was the opposite of the horrible corpse-fruit, or maybe it heightened the impression she made on us. The way she stood there, stooped over, in that red and white tiered skirt and close-fitting black top they all wear, and caught the water from the spout in her cupped hands and drank. The way she straightened up and noticed us, shook her hands dry, and approached us frankly, taking quick, strong steps, slender, but with a well-developed figure, and showing off all the virtues of her appearance to such advantage that Telamon, with his usual lack of self-control, whistled through his teeth and whispered to me: Now there's something nice for you. It hadn't escaped him that I'm susceptible to the charms of brown-skinned, dark-haired girls. But this one here, though poor Telamon wasn't capable of grasping it, this one here was something else. A pulling in all my limbs such as I'd never known, a feeling of absolute enchantment—she's put a spell on me went through my mind, and in fact, so she had. And she wants to keep doing it, Akamas is right about that. And about my having to beware and not let her bamboozle me all the time, because naturally she'll talk about her poor brother's death and spin me one of her tales, so thoroughly believable as long as she's looking you in the eyes, but now I must be on my guard so she won't bamboozle me again.

Of course it was odd, how she greeted us with her hands raised in the sign of peace, a sign proper only to the King or his envoys; how she openly gave her name, Medea, daughter of King Aeëtes and High Priestess of Hecate; how she desired to know our names and our destination, as though it were her right to do so, and I, taken by surprise, revealed to this woman what was meant for the King's ears only. And how unusual the way my heart behaved when I heard my name grow strange in her mouth. It was only much later that we played with the magic of our names . . . today all the old things I haven't thought about for so long are coming back to me. We were on the *Argo*. Medea called me by my name, as though aware of me for the first time, she held me at arm's length and studied me in a way I'd have called more impertinent than captivated, and then she said, very seriously, almost solemnly, as though she'd just made a decision: Jason, I shall eat your heart.

That's the way she was, such affectation. I've never told this to anyone, no one likes to make himself ridiculous. But that night, under that starry sky, I found it—how should I say this—touching. Gods, what a word, Akamas would scowl. As though he hasn't paid her his tribute too. He too. I don't know how far it went—she's always answered such questions, which after all I have a right to ask, by raising her eyebrows—but I'm certainly not blind, I've seen looks passing from him to her, admiration you could call it, or surprise, and with a man like Akamas, who wouldn't show surprise for anything in the world, that must mean something. Maybe jealousy has made me particularly sensitive to that sort of thing. Besides, Akamas's relations with Medea have changed ever since she averted the famine that was threatening Corinth after two years of drought. Not by magic, as the Corinthians claim. In point of fact, she shared her knowledge of edible wild-growing plants, which seems to be inexhaustible, with the Corinthians, and she taught, no, forced them to eat horseflesh. And she forced her Colchians to do so too, as well as us, the few remaining Argonauts. She started with me. Just when food was really scarce, she fixed me a delicious dinner and had me eat it in her presence, face-to-face; I expressed my suspicions, she confirmed them, watched unmoved as I gagged, and then got me, I no longer know how, to declare myself an eater of horsemeat in front of all the people. I was not struck down by wrathful gods, the people slaughtered horses, ate them, survived, and didn't forgive Medea. Since then they consider her an evil woman, because, Akamas says, people would rather believe that they were bewitched than that they devoured weeds and gorged on the entrails of untouchable animals just out of common hunger. Medea says that whoever causes the people to lay hands on what they hold sacred makes himself their enemy. They won't bear it. And so they slander me, she says. But they still haven't built new storehouses.

Too much for me, all these complicated hidden interconnections. In any case, Akamas won't take Medea's part against the charge that she killed her brother. Since all this horse-and-hunger business he considers her a threat to himself. And if anyone has the means of stoking suspicion without directly expressing it, he does.

And it's not as if she makes it easy on a man. You could almost believe she was playing with the danger. Provocative, that's the word. Most Colchian women walk like that. Sure, I like it. But you can also understand the Corinthian wives' complaint: why should foreigners, refugees, be allowed to walk around their city with more self-assurance than they themselves? The upshot was friction, I was supposed to mediate, Medea told me to save my breath.

But where is all this leading me . . . The Fleece? Medea asked, surprised. But why the Fleece? We were standing there by the fountain, she had offered us, Telamon and me, the first pitcher of wine, and for the first time I had seen the sparks in her gray-green eyes, a phenomenon unique in my experience. You can get addicted to them. And when she realizes the effect she's having, she knows how to smile in her superior way and cast her eyes down, releasing the slave from his chains, and to this day it seems to make no difference to her that many of these freedmen hold that superiority very much against her. The Fleece. So now I had to stare into those very eyes and explain to her why I had overseen the building of a mighty ship with fifty oars and a tall mast, manned her with my country's noblest sons, and sailed her through our familiar Mediteranean, through most perilous straits, and into the wild and menacing Black Sea, all the way here to dismal Colchis, where the dead hang on trees, just to fetch a simple ram's skin, which, mind you, as she readily admitted, my Uncle Phrixos, when he was on the run years ago, had handed over here as a present to his hosts. Yes, right. But what reason could I have for reclaiming such a gift? Well, throughout all the days of the voyage it had been very clear to me why we suddenly needed this skin so urgently in Iolcus—after all, we had staked all our energies, to say nothing of our lives, on this enterprise—and now, in front of this woman, I began to stutter, and all my lofty compelling reasons shrank down to the rather pitiful fact that my succession to the throne of Iolcus had been tied to the possession of the Fleece. She questioned us, trying hard to understand. I see, it's a power struggle between two royal houses. Yes. No. Not only. Telamon clumsily came to my aid. He said that my Uncle Pelias, who sat upon the Iolcan throne, had had a dream. How lovely for Pelias, Medea said, she can be disagreeably dry. She said she believed my Uncle Pelias gave me this dangerous task because he simply wanted me out of the country. But no, no. In any case, not only that. Now the problem was to make it clear to this woman that the Fleece wasn't only a pretext but a sacred object that we couldn't do without. How so, she wanted to know. So there we were, called upon to describe the aura of a sacred object in plain words. We dithered zealously until Telamon blurted out, The Fleece is a symbol of manly fruitfulness, whereupon she tersely remarked that Iolcan manly fruitfulness must be in a bad way. I don't like to think about the blustering that Telamon fuddled himself in until she finally cut him off with a negligent wave of her hand.

She got on her high horse, she said she didn't believe her father, the King, would hand over the Fleece just like that, no matter what it might mean to us. She said, A possession considered of little value up to now suddenly becomes precious to a person if another person desires it, don't you think? And thus confused we trotted behind her into her father's palace, which by the way was completely built of wood, skillfully decorated with carvings, certainly, but nobody in our country would call it a palace. Nevertheless, we didn't fail to express our admiration, as befits the guest-friend, though I had difficulty imposing some degree of calm on the swarm of unpleasant thoughts that she had stirred up in my head. That's the way with her to this day. Nothing has so enraged King Creon and his entourage against her as the composure she showed recently when she learned of her expulsion from the palace, allegedly, as the royal physician testified, because her little tonics and potions had harmed the King's aged mother; but no one believed that anyway. Now they're already dredging up other excuses. I've given myself headaches trying to figure out why they wanted her out of the way. Leukon maintained that her natural haughtiness and her derisive manner became too much for the palace to put up with any longer, but is that a sufficient explanation? In any case, she seemed practically relieved as she packed her things—there wasn't much—and I stood around watching her, saying nothing because I had nothing to say. Lyssa was getting the two children ready in the next room, then they were standing in front of me with their parcels, just as when they first moved into this proud palace; I started feeling hot and swallowing hard. I can still hear Medea asking me: Well, are you coming? The idea hadn't occurred to me, and that's exactly what her question was designed to show me. I must have said something like I'd visit her often, her and the children, and she laughed, not scornfully, but rather indulgently, I thought. She let the others go on ahead, stepped close to me, laid her hand on my neck, and said: Don't worry about it, Jason. It had to happen like this.

I can still feel her hand on my neck whenever I want to, and what she said then has often been a comfort to me. But who can I confide that to? Telamon? I haven't been able to make him see reason for a long time. He's never taken a wife, contents himself with transient romances. And he of all people is disgusted with me for not moving into that bird's nest on the palace wall with Medea. He stirs up bad feelings against me in the taverns where he hangs around and drinks up the little money I give him—after all, he's one of the last companions left from our glory days. Sometimes we meet by chance in the shadow of the *Argo,* which was dry-docked near the harbor with great pomp and ceremony and which nobody gives a thought to now; in other words, our deeds have already been forgotten. Once I caught Telamon weeping. He drinks, and that makes a man feel sorry for himself. Akamas is right: the old days become greater the further you move away from them, that's normal, and so it makes no sense to cling to the old days. Fine, but what am I supposed to cling to? Medea? And perish with her? A man could lose his reason.

Colchis would have remained closed to us except for her. She led us to her father, King Aeëtes, who though taken unawares received us; Medea formally presented us to him and went away, despite his bidding her, in commanding tones, to stay. She went away. He sat alone in the great wooden hall, which was richly furnished and decorated with wood carvings. Aeëtes was a frail man, he scarcely filled the royal throne, his face was gaunt and pale, framed by curly black hair—a pile of misery, Telamon said when we were outside again. A different word occurred to me: brittle. His whole appearance was as brittle as the voice he welcomed us with, declaring himself honored to receive guests from so far away, who would surely make known to him the cause of their coming. Not presumptuously, but firmly, I informed him that my mission was to take back to its native land, with his permission, the fleece of the ram that my Uncle Phrixos had brought to Colchis, and thus to strengthen our friendly relations and establish a regular sea route between our two countries.

At first I thought Aeëtes hadn't understood me. Ah yes, yes, Phrixos, he said, and giggled, putting his hand to his mouth with an unseemly, old man's gesture. Then he brought out some silly anecdotes, rather embarrassing tales of my uncle's love affairs, which supposedly went wrong on a regular basis. He talked and talked, girls brought us wine and the delicious barley cakes that I have Colchian women bake for me to this day—none of them does it so well as Lyssa—and then, all at once, he dismissed us without a word about our request. The next evening we were ordered into his presence again, this time with our whole troop, there was a formal reception, as though we hadn't yet met, a different, dignified King sat there in his royal garments surrounded by the Elders of the kingdom, next to me at the table were the dark, reserved Medea and her sister, Chalciope, with her brown skin, her thick shock of blond hair, and her steel-blue eyes. Colchian women can bewilder a man, I thought, beginning to feel comfortable, and then came the cold shower. One of the Elders rose from his seat, produced a raft of meaningless rhetorical flourishes, and finally announced the royal decision. The King was resolved to put me to certain proofs before he would let me have the Fleece. I must overcome the bulls that guarded it, and I must defeat the monstrous serpent under whose protection the Fleece had been hung in the branches of an oak tree in Ares's sacred grove and which, as my men had already learned, was surrounded by the aura of invincibility.

I felt anger rising in me. What was this supposed to mean. Was it a trap. Should I let myself get mixed up in this. I tried to catch the eyes of my men: general cluelessness. If I'd had a choice, I would have jumped to my feet, overturned the table, and left the hall. But we were hopelessly outnumbered.

The serpent. I still dream about it. The Colchian monster-snake that wrapped its monstrous length around the trunk of the oak tree. I see it in my dreams the way my men describe it: three-headed, as thick as the tree trunk, and, it goes without saying, spewing fire. I reserve my opinion on these points, it may be that I failed to notice some details in my battle-frenzy, and the Corinthians want to be told that in the wild east the beasts, too, are horrifying and uncontrollable, and they shudder when you tell them the Colchians kept snakes by their hearths as household gods and fed them with milk and honey. The worthy Corinthians, if they only knew that these foreigners here among us haven't given up this practice, that they keep snakes and feed snakes in secret. But surely no Corinthian would ever set foot in the foreigners' shabby hovels on the edge of the city, nor (as I do) in Medea's dwelling place, where I still go when the urge drives me to her and where a little snake's head with two gold-brown eyes gazes at me from the ashes of Lyssa's hearth until she shoos it away with a light clap of her hands. They know how to tame snakes, that's the truth, I've seen it with my own eyes. I saw how Medea squatted down beside the trunk of that great oak, how the serpent bent toward her and hissed, and how Medea began to hum softly and then to sing a melody that fixed the beast unmoving, so that she was able to drip into his eyes the sap of freshly cut juniper twigs, which she carried in a little flask and which put the dragon, or should I say dragoness, to sleep.

Many times I've had to tell the tale of how I clambered up the tree, how I managed to grab the Fleece and get back down with it successfully, and every time the story has changed a little in accordance with the listeners' expectations, so that they could be properly frightened and properly relieved at the end. Things have reached such a pass that I myself no longer know what I went through with that serpent in the grove and on the oak tree, but no one wants to hear that anymore anyway. In the evenings people sit around campfires and sing about Jason the Dragon-Killer, sometimes I pass by, they couldn't care less. I don't believe they even know that I'm the one they're singing about. Once Medea listened to the songs with me. At the end she said, They've made what they need out of each of us. Out of you, the Hero, and out of me, the Wicked Witch. They've driven us apart like that.

It was a sad moment. And whenever I think about such moments, I just will not believe that she killed her brother. What on earth for? And a small voice inside me says they themselves don't believe it, at least not Akamas, but I've started to be suspicious of my inner voices, it's been explained to me that they were subject to Medea's influence and for all I know they may be still, she has power over people, she entrances them. If her gold-sparkling eyes under the single stroke of her two joined eyebrows look at you long enough, then you'll believe whatever she wants to persuade you of, Creon himself has warned me about that.

King Creon is like a father to me, what am I saying, he's better than my father to me. My father, after all, did give me away when I was still a suckling, perhaps because he wanted to withdraw me from the snares of my uncle, throne-robbing Pelias, and I have no wish to complain about my childhood; with Cheiron to bring him up, a boy could live an unfettered life in the Thessalian mountain forests and still be taught all the knowledge a man of good family needs—I can still remember how my medicinal skills impressed Medea. That was a long time ago. At some point a man must decide what he wants, and he must also be able to forget what he can't use anymore and what's only a burden to him. My father said things like that, he wanted his throne back, that's understandable. He was a stranger to me when I faced him for the first time, and the woman at his side who embraced me amid tears might have been my mother or not. Doubtless that's who she was. A crass woman, in any case. How charming Medea's mother, Eidyia, was in comparison. She sat next to the King, wraith-thin, but not as his shadow. Thin and tough. And highly respected to boot.

Actually we found it excessive, the way the Colchians treated their women, as though something important depended on what they thought and what they said. I could see that Eidyia didn't agree at all with the conditions the King had imposed on me, she was speaking to him with great urgency, but he crept deeper into his royal robes and played deaf. Now we were faced with a choice: we could agree to take on this adventure, which as we well knew could turn dangerous, or we could simply sail away again, leave the Fleece in its place—I was already sick of that stupid pelt—and squirm out of this predicament, making up some story on the way back home. I wasn't very keen on the prospect of winding up as a corpse hanging from the branches of some Colchian oak. There didn't seem to be a third possibility.

It gradually began to dawn on us that we'd barged into a set of circumstances in Colchis, and into one especially delicate area, that we didn't clearly understand. We didn't know the Colchian women. They've always guarded their secrets from foreigners, just as we do. Now I'm saying "we" and I mean the Corinthians, and so Creon's right when he says, But you belong to us, Jason, a blind man can see that. And anyway, we're not belittling the Colchians—I've tried to make this clear to Medea—when we recognize that they're different. She laughed at my efforts in her sneering way, it's getting on my nerves more and more, but she had to admit that the Colchian people here all crowd together in one part of town and cling to their own customs and marry only among themselves. So obviously they think they're different too. Inferior, in the minds of most Corinthians, including King Creon. Jason, please, he told me recently, laying his hand on my arm, when you get right down to it they're just savages. Charming savages, I grant you, it's all too easy to understand why we don't always resist their charms. At times. He smiled mildly. I've got a funny feeling. I believe he wants something specific from me. He's softening you up with gentle blows, Medea says, and then she brushes my cheek with the back of her hand, lightly, as if I were a boy. As if she doesn't reckon with me anymore. Creon reckons with me. I have no idea what I've got to reckon with, and I don't see anyone I could ask, least of all my old companions, the few who followed me here because they had no home to go to or because, like me, they couldn't part with a Colchian girl. They hang out in the taverns by the docks and get on people's nerves with their self-pity. I avoid them. Yes, there was a time when a man knew why he was in the world, but those days are gone.

Now the Corinthians want to examine them, I hear. Or at any rate ask them some questions. To see if they can give any testimony regarding the death of Medea's brother, Apsyrtus. I remonstrated with Akamas, I said to him, Pray tell me, Akamas, what are they supposed to say, and in my heart I thought, for a pitcher of wine they'll say whatever someone wants to hear from them, and Akamas naturally knows this too. So does someone want to hear something specific from them? But that's just too absurd. They'll want to question you too, Jason, Akamas said.

I don't feel good about this, I don't feel good at all. But then what do I know, what could I say? I saw Apsyrtus, right, he was a beautiful, graceful boy with a thin aquiline nose on his swarthy face, and at the banquet table he sat on the left of his father, Aeëtes, who caressed him incessantly, I remember how that repulsed me. Everyone seemed to flatter him, a spoiled princeling sitting secure in his padded nest, I and my kind had it different, we had to fight our way through, but that was just a passing thought, it's amazing that I still remember it. Certainly this young man's misfortune strengthened my impression of him and my vague feeling that from a certain moment on, my fate was bound up with his. The connecting link was Medea. Two days after our reception, two days during which I didn't know what to do, in which no one bestirred himself on our account, the mood in the palace suddenly took a turn for the worse. Everyone seemed terror-stricken, they ran through the corridors speechless and distraught, nobody let himself be spoken to until I came across Chalciope, who was beside herself with grief and, like me, on her way to see Medea. I wanted to get some counsel. That's to say, her name, according to what the Colchians had whispered to my men, meant She of Good Counsel. Well then, let her live up to her name.

She was holed up in a dim chamber and didn't seem like the same woman anymore. She had been crying, now she was motionless, rigid, very pale. She was clutching her arms with her hands as if she had to hold onto herself tight. After a long while she said to me in a lifeless voice: You come at an unfavorable moment, Jason. And much later, as if she were asking herself: Or at an especially favorable one. I didn't dare ask a question. And I became totally superfluous when the Queen entered, Eidyia, livid with anger, at once her two daughters were at her side, holding her, Chalciope waved me off, I came away.

Apsyrtus was murdered, it was said. The poor boy. Dismembered, or so the rumor went. It shook me. Let's just get away, away from here. We started preparations for sailing. Then Medea sent me a message: she wanted to meet with me. In the evening, by the *Argo*. Then she met me there and declared that she'd help me gain the Fleece. She gave no reason. Then she outlined every single step I had to take. How I should seem to renounce the Fleece, seem to prepare for departure, and thus deceive the King. How I should come to the palace for the farewell drink. How she would see to it that neither the palace guards nor those in Ares's grove would disturb me. Why I shouldn't be afraid of the serpent, despite the genuine horror stories she'd just told me about it, and so forth. The entire sequence of events, in every detail. And when we were finished, my head was abuzz, Medea stood up and said, as coolly as she'd said everything else, One condition: you take me with you. And I, caught by surprise, full of conflicting feelings, said simply, Yes. And after I said that, I knew that I'd wanted to, and I felt a strange joy and asked myself whether Medea now expected me to embrace her or make some other meaningful gesture, but she just raised her hand in farewell and slipped away. She behaves like that to this day. If something's important to her, she treats it casually.

Once she did explain something to me seriously—the corpse-fruit. We had to meet several more times, and she noticed how that grove of trees gave me the shivers. She told me that among the Colchians only the women were buried in the earth; that the bodies of the men were hung in trees, where birds could pick their bones clean, and then the skeletons, divided according to families, were placed in rock caves; and that it was an orderly and reverent procedure, what didn't I like about it. The answer to that was more or less everything, but especially the thought of birds pecking apart and devouring a human corpse like any carrion; the dead, I pointed out to her, should be buried physically intact in the earth or walled up in a rock cave, in order to be able to begin the journey through the Underworld and arrive on the Other Side. She countered by asserting that the soul, having escaped unharmed, was no longer present in the body after death, that the Colchians worshiped the souls of the dead in certain places set aside for that purpose, and that the goddess fitted the scattered remains of the dead into new bodies for reincarnation. That, she said, was the firm belief of the Colchians. While she was speaking she observed me narrowly. And doesn't everything depend, she asked in closing, on the significance one gives to an action? The thought was alien to me. I was convinced then and remain so to this day that there's only one right way to honor one's dead, and many wrong ones. Incidentally, she then asked me, I don't know why, whether human sacrifice existed among us in the lands of the setting sun. Of course not, I said indignantly, she tilted her head to one side and looked at me searchingly. No? she said. Not even when the going is toughest? I still answered no, and she said thoughtfully, Well. Maybe that's really true.

And now, after such a long time, she hasn't forgotten our conversation, a little while ago she brushed past me and asked, No human sacrifice, do you still believe that? You poor thing. And she was barely out of sight when that Turon came charging in, the eager creep Akamas has taken into his service, and wanted to know what Medea had said to me. What the hell's going on? This fog they're making me grope around in will yet make me wish I'd never met Medea, or at least that I'd left her and hers behind in Colchis. Yes. Even if the thought scares me. At the same time, I know that without her not one of us would have got out of Colchis alive.

Now the image I've kept below the surface all these years is assaulting me again. The cruelest and most irresistible image of her that I have. Medea as sacrificing priestess before the altar of an ancient goddess of her people, wrapped in a bull's skin, on her head a

Phrygian cap fashioned from bull's testicles, the sign of the priestess entitled to perform sacrifices. And that's what Medea did. Standing at the altar, she brandished the knife over the decorated young bull and slit open the artery in his throat, so that he dropped to his knees and bled to death. But the women caught the blood and drank it, Medea first of all, and I trembled at the sight of her, and I couldn't turn my eyes away, and I'm sure she wanted me to see her like that, frightening and splendid, I desired her as I'd never desired a woman before, I'd never known that such desire existed, it was tearing me apart, and when the blood-frenzied women began stamping their feet in a hideous dance, I fled, and I knew I could never leave Colchis without this woman. I had to have her.

I did everything she commanded me to do. In order to overcome the bulls, I let her put that horrible cap on my head, it had magical powers, she said, and would make me invisible, I let myself be urged on by her savage drum music, which penetrated my limbs and drove me crazy, I no longer knew myself, I leapt among the bulls and slaughtered them, I was beside myself and wanted to be beside myself. I deceived the King and drank a farewell toast to him before he and his attendants dropped off to sleep. I let myself be painted from head to foot with a salve she had, she said it protected against snake venom. I would have believed anything she said. What happened to me next, I don't know. It was atrocious, I know that for sure. My consciousness abandoned me.

When I woke up, I was miserable and sick unto death, she crouched next to me, Medea, it was night, woods all around us, she was stirring a kettle that stood on a tripod over a campfire, the flickering light made her look ages old. I couldn't speak. I had been in the jaws of Death, his breath had brushed me, part of me was still in that other world that we so rightly fear. Without her, without Medea, I would have perished. I must have stammered something like,

Get me out of here, Medea, and she said only, Yes, yes. She scooped out a ladleful of the brew she'd concocted and told me to drink. It tasted abominable and coursed through my veins like fire. Medea laid her hand on my chest for a long time, and in so doing generated a whirling in me that gave me back my life. It's the most wondrous thing I've ever experienced, I said, this should never stop. And then at some point I murmured, You're a sorceress, Medea, and she, unfazed, said simply, Yes. I arose from that bed rejuvenated and full of strength. I had no sense of the time that had passed. Since that moment I understand the reverence and respect that Medea received from her Colchians.

And I also understand Akamas and the people of Corinth, who want to get rid of her. Get rid of her? Where do such wicked words come from, they're nonsense, I must forget them. Not too long ago, after watching me with his all-too-subtle talent for observation as I was being tossed between my devotion to Medea and my duty—and pleasure—to be of service to King Creon, Akamas then vilely suggested that I simply join my Argonauts in the taverns, or go with one of these whores, in order to relax, and that made me so furious I very nearly took him by the throat in the middle of the Corinthian marketplace. And he? What did he say? That's good too, he said unmoved, you need to let off steam, Jason. I turned around and left him standing there. Something's going wrong, very wrong, and I can't make it stop.

If she just wasn't so arrogant. After all, she was the fugitive, and I was her only resort. With the help of the Golden Fleece, I planned to bring about my father's restoration to his royal dignity, but after that had failed, and after I, too, had to flee my homeland, Iolcus, then the grace of King Creon was *our* only resort. I've had to tell her that again and again. And what's her response? I didn't leave Colchis to come and cower here, that's the kind of thing she says, and she refuses to bind up that wild bush of hair as married Corinthian women do, and further says, So what? Don't you find me more beautiful like this? Shameless. Knows exactly what I find beautiful and who I think the most beautiful. And runs through the streets like bad weather and screams when she's angry, and laughs out loud when she's happy. I just realized, it's been a long time since I heard her laugh. But there was one thing she didn't let them take away from her, she would still dash through the city with her little wooden casket and the white band around her forehead, signs that she was on a healing mission and wished to concentrate her thoughts undisturbed, and everyone respected her, and the families whose members she'd helped spread her praise. It became the fashion in Corinth to consult her rather than the astrologers or the physicians from Akamas's school. The wretched woman got so carried away that she referred to the healing skills of those worthy gentlemen as "bleak magic" in conversation with one of the King's officials, whose son she had cured of unbearable headaches, and who most dutifully reported her quip to the palace. After that we had our first serious quarrel. Watch what you say! I yelled at her, and she, with that provoking calmness of hers, replied that she was about to make the same recommendation to me. I said, They're sick of you, and she said, We'll see about that. Then she said, Listen, there was a time when you knew better yourself. What did your Cheiron teach you, then? The kind of stupid tricks they use to pull the wool over people's eyes? It was strange. I was beginning to forget what Cheiron had taught me, the genuine healing arts that Medea practices. They're of no use to me here. Here I have to keep abreast of what's going on in the palace, and she refuses to grasp that.

Of course they were sick of her. She had to clear out of the rooms we shared in one of the side wings of the palace. I was assured that this measure wasn't directed at me. But didn't I agree that anyone whose emanations could possibly cause illness should be kept at a safe distance from the royal family? If they were acting two-faced and lying and cobbling together false pretexts just to get her out of the palace, they must have considered it a serious matter. Naturally she was waiting for me to defend her. But how can you defend someone against trumped-up charges? And if I had gone with her, I would only have made our situation worse.

She went. She was given two of Akamas's men as an escort, assigned to prevent her from cursing the palace. When I took Akamas to task about this, he burst into raucous laughter. Oh these simple minds, he cried out, vastly amused. As if someone like Medea couldn't curse whomever and whatever she pleased, without words and under any guard's nose.

At first I visited Medea regularly in her clay hut. Granted, it wasn't the same between us anymore, but that's normal, I see that everywhere around me. Creon has drawn me closer to him, all sorts of duties and services have been imposed on me, some of them most prestigious, the kind that exalt one's person. The Fleece is lying under many other sacrificial offerings on the altar of Zeus and moldering. My prospects in Corinth aren't bad, I've got my own ideas about that. Akamas drops the odd hint. Everything could go quite smoothly if only they hadn't dug up this old story about Medea killing her brother. So what if she did? At this late date, what harm can that do anyone? But many seem to think it can do them good, all too many, I can't hide that from myself.

What on earth shall I do. Only she, Medea, could advise me. There's a crazy idea.

Three

Agameda

MEDEA: For women, though inept at
doing good,
Are brilliant fashioners of every
evil.

EURIPIDES, *Medea*

I've done it. I've seen her grow pale. I wasn't expecting the right words when they came, but my hatred has labored over them for so many months that they were ready at the right moment. Medea blanched. I saw her lift her hands, as though she would beseech me. Naturally she didn't do that, she tried to compose herself. She would have got a laugh and a sneer for her pains. Or would she? Wouldn't I have shamed her more by being magnanimous?

Often it hangs on a thread, how a matter is going to proceed. Back then, for example, a long time ago, when she betrayed me, yes, betrayed, whether she'll admit it or not, such memory lapses she allows herself. Or a short time ago, when she was sick. As if she'd foreseen the approaching disaster. I'd have gladly been the first to announce it to her. I'd have watched her gladly, too gladly, to see how she received the news, and I'd have reveled in her terror. I was furious when I realized how high her fever was. How she was simply escaping by way of her illness. At the same time I understood that she needed help, Medea, the great healer, she was lying there helpless, my heart leaped, finally my most secret wish would come true, the great theme of my childhood, that I, I would become her healer, would hover around her sickbed, care for her, serve her, make myself indispensable, and finally I'd receive what I so horribly craved, her gratitude. Her love. I despised myself for that, but the moment that used to dominate my daydreams and my nightdreams had come. She needed me. I'd rescue her. She'd be bound to me by eternal gratitude; now I'd live in her society as her favorite, preferred above all others.

There it was again. The intoxication that overcomes me when I'm in Medea's presence overcame me—but for the last time. Now I know I'm safe. Safe from her damned tricks and her famous emanations, that's what I flung at Lyssa when she came sweeping in and shooed me away from Medea's bed with gestures of abhorrence—I won't forget that—as though I were the one who had wished this sickness on her.

I. Agameda. Who was once her most gifted pupil, she told me so herself. You'll become an excellent healer, Agameda. But as usual she managed to put a damper on my mounting joy right away: When you learn to efface yourself. I don't heal, she said, and neither do you, Agameda, something heals with our help. What we can do is make sure that this something is able to flourish freely, in our patients and in ourselves. Well, yes. I've copied and learned from her most of her methods, the ingredients of the various stocks and how to prepare them, the properties of herbs, many of her magic formulas. I have become a Healer. Many people consult me rather than her because she scares them. From the beginning noble Corinthian families, no less, would call me into their well-furnished houses, quite happy to listen while I sincerely marveled at their homes and told them about the primitive accommodations in which most people in Colchis live. They found it hard to believe that even the royal palace was built of wood, and they pitied me, and the more they pitied me the better they paid me and the higher opinion they could have of their own way of life—I figured that out before long, and before long

I had the clothes I wanted and the fine foods I was getting used to, likewise the sweet, heavy wine they drink here. Presbon, who has by now celebrated many triumphs with the festival productions he puts on for the Corinthians, Presbon has been recommending me to his friends. And now that Medea's star is about to set and I'm becoming quite the fashion in the palace, as Presbon says, now when I leave a patient I often find a piece of jewelry in my pocket. A ring, a necklace. I don't wear them yet, Presbon talked me out of doing that. One shouldn't provoke other people's envy. He, Presbon, doesn't envy me, I'm no rival of his, it can only be to his advantage if he's not the sole Colchian winning honors in Corinth. At first he didn't deign to look at me, I wasn't the kind of woman that excites him, that is, beautiful and blindly devoted to him, two things that I know I am not. But now he looks at me, I find, with a kind of astonishment that can stand in for desire. That can become desire. If I know anything about the strangeness of manly desire, it's that, and I can't put it often enough to the test.

Naturally that shrew Lyssa threw a tantrum, told Presbon and me we were despicable, and stopped just short of calling us traitors, as they surely do among themselves, these prematurely aging Colchians, when they're hunkered down together. When they're on the main square in their quarter, which they've turned into a Little Colchis and insulated against any sort of change, and they stick their heads together and whisper stories to one another, stories about a wondrous Colchis that has never existed anywhere on this earth. It would be laughable if it weren't so sad, I shouted at Lyssa. You see only what you want to see, was her rejoinder, only those few old fossils who've jerry-built themselves a dreamworld out of pure grief and homesickness, and out of rage at the treatment they get from the Corinthians. Then this woman dared to tell me I've always made it easy on myself, I've always patched together an image of others and especially of myself to suit what I needed and what I could bear. I was beside myself. Me? I screamed back at her. Me? And what about your infallible Medea? Who surrounds herself only with her admirers? Who doesn't let anyone else get close to her? Then Lyssa got quiet. You really are crazy, she said. You really believe what you say. You really want to destroy her.

Yes. That *is* what I want. The day when it happens will be my happiest day.

Lyssa the cow, that's what Presbon calls her. Born to suckle. First there was Arinna, her own daughter, and then she also took Medea's two sons to her breast, making what contribution she could so that this woman, Medea, would be happy in everything she did. So that she sat there as though in a fortress made of happiness. She carried her wild mass of hair through the city like a banner. But those days are gone forever. Now when she goes to the palace, which is seldom enough, she wraps a cloth around her hair. Jason publicly disavows her and goes to see her on the sly. Oh yes, I keep informed. I stood in front of Lyssa and sneered, Medea doesn't need anyone to destroy her, she's taking care of that herself, and doing a thorough job. Then she grabbed me by the shoulder and shook me; I must tell Presbon, when she's angry her eyes aren't cowlike at all. She'd had enough of my coy hints, she screamed. And just in time the thought occurred to me that I should stop. I snatched her hand off me and left.

Everything had been decided. I was ready. Presbon was waiting for me. We had to go to Akamas. It was time for our wishes to become reality.

If we thought Akamas would welcome us, we were totally mistaken. Akamas made us wait. Sent word that he was busy. Quick to take offense, I tried to leave, but Presbon held me back. He said that we owed it to our hosts to inform them about anything that endangered their community. Presbon is a person endowed with the gift of self-deception. He knows only the noblest motives for whatever he does or doesn't do. But I think I'm gradually seeing through the real reasons behind his eagerness to betray Medea. Presbon doesn't just want to be loved the way we all do. He can feel properly important only when a great crowd is admiring him, so he organizes their festivals, it doesn't matter whether he believes in their gods or not. He makes himself believe in them. He thinks Medea despises him because of that. The reality is much worse: she's indifferent to him. That must be an unbearable thorn in his side, and I've placed in his hands the means of pulling out that thorn once and for all.

Akamas received us with the same ineffable reserve that the Corinthians have practiced toward us Colchians from the beginning; no matter how close one of us thinks he or she has got to them, that reserve can never be overcome. For they were born with the unshakable conviction that they're superior to people who are short of stature and brown of skin, who live in villages on the fringes of their city, and among whom the legend persists that they're the original inhabitants, the first to settle the shores of this sea, the first to catch fish in these waters and plant olive trees in this soil. Naturally they drew us Colchians to their side, naturally they wanted to admit us into their settlements as people of their own kind, naturally they offered our men their daughters, our girls their sons. They would have most preferred to stir us down into the shapeless, faceless mash, into this jumble of tribes and peoples, and indeed there were some Colchians, exhausted after long wandering, robbed of their power to resist, who succumbed to this temptation, flung themselves into the arms of these inferior stocks, dissolved into them, and thus ceased to be Colchians. I, too, find it senseless to cling to an untenable self-image, but why not make an effort to rise into the higher form of existence? I don't want to be nobody. With this goal in mind, at last I stood face-to-face with Akamas.

Akamas was courteous in his impersonal way. He said not a

word about our long wait, but made a formal bow and then at Presbon's request even sent Turon, his clever young assistant, out of the room. He passed quite close to me and gave me a wink. We know one another very well; Turon is one of the young Corinthian men to whom I don't refuse myself, because they will gain influence and might be useful to me sometime.

In contrast to Colchis, in Corinth it's imperative for the man to speak first, even (a ridiculous custom) for the man to speak for the woman. Presbon, therefore, began talking first and, as is his custom, walked a fine line between presumption and obsequiousness. He let Akamas know that I, Agameda, had an important statement to make. Akamas turned his gaze to me. He said: Speak. I said the matter concerned Medea. Akamas curtly interrupted me, saying that immigrants were not his responsibility. I swore to myself he'd learn to respect me yet. I coolly said that he naturally had to decide for himself whether he wanted to hear information whose importance for Corinth it was not up to us to judge. Thereupon he looked me in the eye more narrowly, surprised, it seemed to me, and repeated imperiously: Speak. I told him what I had seen, that Medea had been spying on Queen Merope at the King's banquet.

The man disliked hearing this. Spying? he asked with raised eyebrows. But how, my dear. My body grew coarse under his impudent gaze, my big nose that I try never to show in profile, my great rawboned hands and feet that I've tried to hide ever since I was a girl. Only Medea, to whom for a long time I revealed, to my shame, my deepest secrets, tried to persuade me of my beauties: my well-formed eyebrows, my thick hair, my breasts. But my hair is too lank, my breasts are slack, anyone can see that, Akamas saw it; and I cursed Presbon for bringing me here. Akamas despised me. That wasn't a new experience for me. My worthy Colchians despise me too, ever since I started appearing less and less frequently in their little colony and letting myself be seen more and more in the company of influential Corinthians, and more than ever after I happened to mention that I'd found Colchis insufferable for a long time and saw no reason to cultivate its memory. Well, you did a brilliant job of hiding your feelings back then, Lyssa once said to me. And what of it? I couldn't care less about that, as long as the Corinthians are grateful for my bluntness. I figured out early on how urgently they need their belief that they live in the most perfect land under the sun. What does it cost me to strengthen that belief?

Akamas, however, will have to pay for letting me feel his contempt. I, too, want to intervene in the destinies of others, I'm as gifted as he is when it comes to that, and no pleasure exceeds the satisfaction that wells up in me when I've so thoroughly imbued another with my ideas and my intentions that he considers them his own.

Conveniently enough, what I had to report to Akamas corresponded to the truth. By chance—that was the only detail in my report that wasn't true—by chance, while standing near the exit during the King's banquet in accordance with my instructions as the person in charge of Princess Glauce, I saw our Queen Merope leave the hall. Alone. And then I observed how Medea followed her, practically on her heels. How first the Queen and then Medea disappeared behind an animal skin hanging on the wall of a side passage and for a long time, in any case as long as I thought it proper to wait, did not reappear. So that I became concerned and would have sounded an alarm if Glauce's dizzy spell hadn't required my entire attention. But he knew that already. Dizzy spell, that's the expression the physicians have agreed with the King to use when his thin pale daughter once again begins to twitch and throws herself to the ground, where her body contorts itself hideously and seems as taut as though strung on a bow, while her eyes roll back so that only the whites can be seen and foam hangs on her distorted lips. Everyone in the hall witnessed this embarrassing incident, including Akamas, including Presbon, who watched as one of his grandiose spectacles meant to glorify the royal house came to such an unfortunate and untimely end. I, however, had to sprinkle the unhappy girl with water, had to hold her wildly thrashing head still, and finally had to run alongside the litter on which she was carried back to her chambers, where I sought to bring her back to herself with the help of herb poultices and certain palpations. While I was doing this, I had to be frightfully careful to give precedence to the royal physicians—a helpless lot, by the way—and to avoid any later mention of my part in poor Glauce's rehabilitation.

Only the severity and urgency of the interrogation Akamas subjected me to made me realize how seriously he took the report I'd given him. Made me realize what danger Medea had brought upon herself. The notion pleased me, only she must not at any price draw me into this danger with her. I needed all my powers of persuasion to satisfy Akamas that I hadn't followed the two women for so much as a step and didn't have the least idea what was concealed behind the skins hanging in the side passage. I hope for your sake that's true, he snapped, but I could tell that he believed me. But later Presbon gave me something to think about, pointing out that belief or disbelief would count for nothing with Akamas if he should decide to drag me into Medea's downfall; for his questions must have made it clear even to me that this was a matter of life and death. The weight we'd laid across Medea's shoulders was heavier than we had thought. If I had known that, I ask myself, would I still have gone to Akamas, and the answer stands before me clearly: Yes. Still, even then. And even if that weight would crush me along with her.

But it certainly will not, Akamas himself will prevent it. He needs me, and not only in the coarse sense that became apparent to

me on the spot. Naturally he needed me as a witness, because nobody could perform that role more believably than I. He let me play
the part that suits me so well. He needed me for the net Medea
caught herself in before she knew it was there. I was at Akamas's
service in this, I made myself indispensable. It soon dawned on me,
however, that another effect I had on him was more important, he
abandoned himself to it, and now he can no longer do without it.
Medea in her blindness puts her faith in people's strengths, I put
mine in their weaknesses. And so, though his body's a bit too small
and has turned out a bit too unsightly, though his head's a bit too
large and has turned out a bit too round, with slightly protruding
goggle eyes, still I've coaxed and kindled desires in him that he
wouldn't admit to himself, and like any man who's repressed desires
too long, he has inevitably become addicted to them. I don't mean
love in its various playful forms, Akamas was proof against those. I
mean the craving to be uninhibitedly wicked, which of course often
expresses itself in love play.

Not with Akamas. He is a man put together out of strangely
dissimilar parts. He lives hidden inside carefully crafted edifices of
ideas, which he takes for reality but which have no purpose other
than to buttress his easily shaken self-confidence. He will brook no
opposition, he arrogantly heaps scorn, both veiled and overt, upon
less intelligent people, and therefore over everyone, for he must be
superior to all. I remember the moment when it became clear to me
that he knows little of human nature and that in order to live he
must rely on a supporting framework of principles that no one dare
question; otherwise, he feels intolerably threatened. One of these
principles is his fixed idea that he is a just man. I could scarcely
believe that he was serious, but when he started bringing up all the
points in Medea's favor, I understood that it would perfectly suit his
convenience to receive tangible proofs against Medea. That he was

sick and tired of the airs she put on. That he was fed up with having to answer her infallibility with equal infallibility so that he wouldn't feel inferior in her presence. Oh, I've done a thorough study of all the ways that woman can affect people.

Had I been wrong, I could have lost everything, but when Akamas began to praise Medea's good qualities I interrupted him by asking if he believed what he was saying. Presbon, as he later confessed to me, caught his breath. Akamas is the King's closest adviser, and no one had ever spoken to him with such effrontery.

Akamas stopped in the middle of his sentence, I saw a flash of surprise in his eyes, as well as the interest I had hoped to arouse. What did I mean, he wanted to know. I said that when a person acts so perfect and beyond reproach as Medea does, then that must mean that there's a rotten spot somewhere. That she has something to hide after all. That she gives others a bad conscience by way of making sure no one looks behind the beautiful veil she's drawn around herself. He, Akamas, must know that very well.

Akamas was silent. Then he said to Presbon: This is certainly a clever young thing you've brought me. Almost too clever, don't you think. The business was still touch-and-go, until I fell back on a method that, as I've confirmed again and again, works on every man: I flattered him shamelessly. I'm no cleverer than anyone else, I said, and certainly not so clever as he. Sometimes, though, I was fortunate, I got to show someone important to me his own cleverness.

Since then, Presbon admires me boundlessly. I believe he didn't dare to sleep with me for a long time after that because he felt inferior to me. And, naturally, because he didn't want to be poaching on Akamas's land. Because sometimes, on evenings when we've discussed some particular plans, it's happened that I've spent the night with him. Well, yes. A man probably can't be outstanding in all areas, I don't insist on that. It's easy for me to make Akamas think he's an unsurpassable lover. No one else could give me a greater thrill than I feel while lying next to the shrewdest and most powerful man in this city.

That's the way things are now, and the best part is that nobody can be sure they'll stay that way. Everything's hanging in the balance, that's what I enjoy the most, every day is a leap into unknown waters, every day challenges me to the uttermost. For naturally Akamas is on his guard against me, and naturally I'm on my guard against him, and naturally I know that the part of his soul he loves the most is still inclined toward Medea, and that therefore he's working against her with one hand, the one that belongs to the King, while with the other, the one he carries to his heart when he bows to her, he's trying to offset the disaster he's preparing for her. Maybe that's calculated too, that would be just like him, and after all he succeeded in keeping her trust for a long time. Besides, I feel there's still something else at the bottom of Akamas's inscrutable relationship with Medea, something barely nameable. If I call it a bad conscience, I miss the mark, and yet I've noticed something not only about Akamas but also about other Corinthians, something that unites them with one another more than their ruling house, without their suspecting it. In some subterranean unprovable way, their forefathers' knowledge seems to have been transmitted to these latecoming descendants, the knowledge that once upon a time they conquered this land by brute force from its original inhabitants, whom they despise. I've never heard anyone in Corinth speak about this, but one night a casual remark from Akamas suddenly made it clear to me what Medea provides for him without knowing it: she enables him to prove to himself that he can be just, unprejudiced, and friendly to a barbarian too. Absurdly enough, these qualities have become fashionable at court, but it's different with the common people, who display their hatred of the barbarians without restrictions and without pangs of conscience. The task of bringing Akamas to the point of working unreservedly against Medea spurs me on.

At our first meeting he had made it clear to us, in the most arrogant way he's capable of, that severe punishment would be our lot should we fail to hold our curiosity in check and try to discover what's hidden behind the pelt behind which I saw first Merope and then Medea disappear. We took the sacred oath willingly, and since I'm not tired of living I've kept that oath up to now and will keep it forever. All three of us privately hoped that Medea would do something stupid, and so she has. She's been snooping around, cautiously, it's true, but whoever looks for evidence of her actions can find it. The secret she's trying to track down, however, seems to be so appalling that this evidence cannot be used against her publicly. Akamas outlined the situation for us in a few convoluted sentences. We grasped it at once, and it was Presbon who came up with the idea of finding another offense instead of the one we weren't allowed to charge her with, one that could be employed against her publicly and would in addition lead to the desired result. We spoke not a syllable about what this desired result might be. We made a game of our plans, which grew more and more refined, and played it in an unreal atmosphere, as though no one could be affected by our playing. If one wishes to think freely and effectively at the same time, this is a very useful method. It's a kind of thinking, moreover, that we in Colchis haven't yet recognized, and supposedly given only to men; but I know I have a talent for it. Only I practice it in secret.

Akamas gave us no instructions, he wanted to keep open the possibility of a retreat. Wanted to place Medea under observation for a little while. Wanted to see whether she wouldn't come to her senses all by herself. But I was positive she wouldn't just stop making unobtrusive inquiries here and there concerning the passageway into which she had followed the Queen—meanwhile I'd come to know this much, but I was not permitted to know it. I could rely on Medea's fancying herself untouchable. She ran around as though under some protective covering. I on the other hand have been without protection since early childhood, exposed to every sort of injury. She couldn't even imagine such a thing, Medea, the King's daughter, Medea, Hecate's Priestess. Yes, at the age of ten, after my mother died, I was placed among the servant girls in the temple and allowed to study under Medea; ever since I could think, that had been my most fervent wish. Medea's way of life seemed to me the only one worth striving for, and so, when my mother died, I couldn't feel only sorrow. Medea had been her friend, had summoned up all her skills to rescue her, but the fever burned her alive. I had never before seen Medea so angry when one of her patients died. There was something unseemly about her anger, for every Colchian knows that the human ability to heal operates within limits beyond which the gods take matters into their own hands. It is not fitting to offend the gods by excessively mourning the dead, as the Corinthians do to our dismay; but they of course lack the certainty that the souls of the dead, after a period of repose, rise again in new bodies.

In any case, Medea kept her promise to my mother and admitted me into her group of pupils. She taught me what she knew, but to my disappointment she kept me at a distance, she withdrew the affection the child was yearning for, and it wasn't until much later, when I was promoted to the first rank of the class, that she said to me once, in passing, surely I had understood, she'd had to treat me more strictly than all the others so that nobody could accuse her of favoring me over them. That's when I began to hate her.

She told me once, You can't have everything. Well, she, too, was to learn that you can't have everything, the secure place in the temple and everyone's love at the same time. She didn't notice it at all. Only here in Corinth did she start paying attention to me again, after I'd broken away from the worthy, boring Colchians and begun mingling with the young people of Corinth. Once she sought me out, feigned sympathy, and asked me if I was unhappy. I only laughed. It was too late.

Unhappy. Gone are the days when she could make me unhappy. As though the thing is to be happy. Turon and I, we suit each other splendidly because neither of us tries to put anything over on the other. A practical alliance, Presbon says, he understands that, and it doesn't exclude still other liaisons. All of a sudden they all want me. As a man, Presbon is rather repulsive, with his unmanageable red hair and his bloated body. He needs someone who'll listen to him, he gets more pleasure from his own verbal effusions than from sleeping with a woman. His vanity is boundless, he has no control over it, my exaggerated praise excites him more than my body does, I know it. And why on earth not? Every woman uses whatever gifts she has to bind a man to herself. Turon has opened for me the way into the royal household, Presbon is showing me the way to avenge myself on Medea. For naturally it was he who made the proposal which we then developed together in meticulous detail over the course of a long night, and at the end of that night we slept together lustily. The plan was brilliant, because it kept all possibilities open. Medea would be accused of having killed her brother, Apsyrtus, in Colchis. This would give Akamas an excuse to proceed against her whenever he wanted to, since he couldn't make use of her real offense: having penetrated one of Corinth's most intimate secrets. Neither of us, by the way, neither Presbon nor I, made any attempt to conceal from the other our gloating delight over this, that Corinth, too, so wonderful, rich, self-confident, and arrogant, has its underground passages where secrets are buried deep. Ordinary people with weaknesses live better lives among other people who have their weaknesses too.

We couldn't let Akamas get wind of this. Our best course was to humor him with certain complicated facts, around which his way of thinking got itself tangled only too happily. When he asked us whether Medea had really murdered her brother, we gave the answer we'd agreed upon: that in any case this rumor, then current in Colchis, had never been disproved, Medea herself had never denied it. Akamas began thinking aloud in order to give us the opportunity to allay his objections. But all that happened so long ago (he mused), and actually it concerns only the Colchians. But they, mind you, were under the protection of the King of Corinth, who presumably would not deny them his help should they demonstrate the grave necessity of wiping out old wrongs at long last. Still (he went on), such a step requires thorough consideration. He must be able to rely on our keeping this matter an absolute secret from everyone. He said that last part menacingly. We both knew that any change in this situation favorable to Medea would put us in danger. We have a powerful interest in the worsening of Medea's position. Akamas knows this. He despises himself and us because his interests are the same as ours, we know that, and he knows that we know it. Our relations are gradually becoming unfathomable, and that's what I enjoy. Clear-cut relations bore me to death.

Now all we needed to do was to keep our eyes open. Medea was walking into the net step by step, the only thing we had to concern ourselves with was making certain that Akamas learned about each of those steps—not from us, of course—and that it became clear to him Medea wasn't giving up. Cautiously, it's true, but no less persistently, she was carrying on her investigations, slowly but surely gaining access to all the people in Corinth she thought could give her some information about the hidden discovery she must have made in that underground passage. I have a hunch as to its nature, but I'm on my guard not to let so much as a single word about this matter escape me. Not even in my deepest depths, in my heart of hearts, do I allow myself to put my hunch into words. And sometimes I simply cannot believe the thoughtless way she's acting.

She hasn't shrunk from holding secret meetings with the Queen in that old part of the palace that everyone else avoids. When Akamas learned of this—this time with no assistance from us, he has his own sources—I finally saw him in a rage. Now he couldn't protect Medea anymore, he said. And he couldn't go on expecting us to keep our knowledge to ourselves. It was a moment divided between terror and joy.

Both of us, Presbon and I, agreed to tell only one person each about the suspicions against Medea. We were curious about how fast the rumor would spread. After two days, all the Colchians knew about it, but only a few Corinthians, who actually seemed little inclined to pay attention to old, unpalatable Colchian affairs. Jason, of course, flew into a panic at once. But, to my natural satisfaction, even Medea seems to have felt the blow. Although she couldn't possibly have known who started the rumor, she considered it appropriate to challenge me in the middle of the street. Just listen, Agameda, she said straight out, you know very well that I had nothing to do with Apsyrtus's death. Then I had one of my brilliant inspirations. I said: And you, Medea, should know that a sister can have her brother on her conscience in different ways.

That's when she turned pale, I saw it.

Four

Medea

Apsyrtus, brother, so you're not dead then, I gathered up your little bones in vain, one by one, from that night-shrouded field where the frenzied women had scattered you, poor piecemeal brother. You've come after me, tenacious as I never knew you to be—but then, how did I know you—you've put your piecemeal limbs back together, gathered them up from the seafloor, bone by bone, and you've followed me as a thing of air, as a rumor. You never wanted to be powerful, and now you are. Powerful enough to fetch me to your side, in the air or on the seafloor, at least that's what they believe, not only Presbon and Agameda, who desire it so urgently, but also Leukon, I saw the worry in his eyes. I, on the other hand, barely gave a start when the rumor's forerunners first appeared in the distance, indeed, no one said anything to my face, they whispered behind my back. I heard your name, after so long a time, once again, your name, and then mine, and if I spun around suddenly, all I saw were sealed faces and cast-down eyes. Everybody knew already, except for me, at last Lyssa enlightened me: I was supposed to have killed you, Apsyrtus, my brother. I laughed. Lyssa didn't laugh. I looked at her, and then I said, But you know the real story. I know it, Lyssa said, and I'll always know it. That meant that not all who knew would always know what they knew. I still didn't understand,

I even had a feeling that was rather like relief, simply because something was happening, and through it perhaps the boredom that over the years in Corinth had settled in me like a murky sediment might be dissolved.

Corinth, along with everything that had happened and was happening in it, had nothing to do with me. But at home, our Colchis had become like an expanded part of my own body—I could sense its every movement. My premonition of Colchis's fall was like an insidious disease in me, I'd lost all appetite, I told you that, little brother, you were so understanding, so sensitive. When we'd sit around with Mother, with Chalciope, with Lyssa, and go over what was happening in Colchis and how it worried us, you were still a child, but you saw things so clearly. Nothing has tormented me more than thinking you may have foreseen that it would cost you your life when our father, when the King, took you and us by surprise and uncovered that damned plot of ours. When we could come up with no better defensive measures than a vague uneasiness. We had underestimated him, our frail, incompetent father had focused his last remaining little scrap of strength on a single point: to keep himself in power and therefore alive. That kind of cunning, that willingness to go to any extreme, was new to us, and we didn't recognize it. We were blind, Apsyrtus.

Even you had understood that the way Aeëtes ruled Colchis was setting more and more Colchians against him, including our mother and me, Priestess of Hecate, whose temple became, without any effort on my part, a meeting place for dissenters, especially the younger people; and you, little brother, were always there. They disapproved of Aeëtes's stubbornness, of the court's useless magnificence, and demanded that the King use our country's treasure, our gold, to spur our trade and improve the miserable lives of our farmers. They wanted the King and his clan to be mindful of the duties that had fallen upon the ruling class from time immemorial in Colchis. Ah, Apsyrtus! The things that we in our ignorance considered magnificence! Since I've been in Corinth, I've come to know what a display of magnificence is, but here nobody is upset by it, even the poor people in the villages and by the roadside go into raptures when they talk about the great palace banquets, for which they have to hand over their livestock and their grain without ever catching so much as a reflection of one of these feasts.

We in Colchis were inspired by the ancient legends of our land, where just Queens and Kings ruled, where the people lived in harmony with one another, and where property was so evenly distributed that no one envied anyone else or schemed to take his possessions or his life. During my early days in Corinth, before I learned my lesson, every time I spoke of this Colchian dream the same expression crossed my listeners' faces, a mixture of disbelief and compassion turning to aversion and disgust, so that I gave up trying to explain that this ideal was so tangible to us Colchians that we measured our lives by it. We'd seen how we were getting further from it year after year, and our old, ossified King was the chief hindrance. It was an easy step to the notion that a new King could bring about a change. The women who belonged to our circle conceived the bold idea of making our sister, Chalciope, the new Queen. Tradition has it that in earlier times there were Queens in Colchis, and since we were now in the process of restoring the old ways to their former importance, some of the oldest of our companions reminded us that formerly a King was allowed to reign in Colchis for only seven years, or at the most for another seven years after that; then his time was up, and he had to relinquish his office to his successor. We figured it out: we were in the seventh year of King Aeëtes's second period of rule, and there were some credulous ones among us who considered it possible that Aeëtes, if only we could convince him he'd be acting in obedience to an old Colchian law, would voluntarily step aside.

How stupid we were. How blind. Aeëtes knew the old tales too, naturally someone informed him of what we planned to do. We had underestimated him. When the group of Colchians we'd sent appeared before him, he was prepared. Instead of receiving their announcement that his reign had come to an end, he surprised them with a long-winded account of the old custom according to which a King was allowed to hold sway for no more than twice seven years, followed by a pompous declaration that he would bow to this custom; he would, furthermore, do exactly what his forefathers had done: he'd put aside his rank for one day, and for that day his son and future successor, Apsyrtus, would be King in Colchis. This would, he declared, more than satisfy the traditions of our people, for surely we wouldn't go so far as to demand adherence to the oldest rituals, which required that either the King or his young proxy be sacrificed.

The people were transformed from claimants into supplicants whose power of speech failed them before they withdrew in embarrassment. Perhaps we might have reacted with more presence of mind were it not that during those very days the Argonauts were everywhere, prowling around, getting in our way, and we had to work to divert their attention. They didn't notice anything. The King took advantage of the situation, he acted swiftly and shrewdly. With appropriate but not exaggerated ceremony, he renounced his crown and installed you, my poor brother, as King. I can still see you, enveloped in sumptuous garments, a tiny figure on the massive wooden throne, and next to you, unassuming, in simple clothing, Aeëtes, the King-no-more. I didn't understand what was going on, that's my only excuse, but I was seized by the apprehension I saw written on your face.

I still don't know exactly how he did it. Maybe he didn't have to do very much at all. Maybe, in the beginning, he didn't intend to do anything other than what he'd said to us and formed the idea of killing you, or letting you be killed, only later, when it became clear to him that his tricky maneuvering wouldn't solve his problem. And afterward, maybe he wasn't even faking his grief for his son. If he could have had it both ways, if he could have stayed in power and kept you alive, he would have been glad to do both, brother. The moment when he recognized that both weren't possible must have been horrible for him. But then, true to his nature, he chose power. And, as a means to power, intimidation.

Maybe one of his minions gave a sign to those women, that fanatical band of old crones whose purpose in life was to oblige us in Colchis to live just as our ancestors had done, down to the smallest detail. We didn't take them seriously, that was a mistake; all at once there came into existence in Colchis a distribution of power that was favorable to those women, so that they believed their time had come. Delighted by the King's revival of the old laws, now they wanted to see them followed to all their conclusions, for only one of the two, the King or his proxy, could survive, and when it was midnight and your day as King ended, brother, they passed through an entrance that on that night, oddly enough, wasn't guarded—as they, oddly enough, knew—and burst into your chambers, where they were able to find you defenseless in your bath and kill you, singing their bloodcurdling songs all the while. Such was the custom in the olden days, to which we, too, had appealed because we thought they promised us an advantage. And ever since I shudder at the thought of those old days and the forces they released in us, forces we could then no longer control. At some point this killing of the proxy King, which everyone approved of, including the victim himself—at some point this must have turned into murder, and if your fearful death has taught me anything, brother, it's that we can't deal with the fragments of the past any way we like, piecing them together or ripping them apart just to suit our convenience. And insofar as I didn't prevent that, and even promoted it, then to that extent I was an accomplice in your death. Agameda meant something else when she accused me recently, but I still turned pale. I blanch every time I think about you, brother, and about this death that drove me away from Colchis. Agameda has no idea. Hates me blindly. But why does she hate me. Why am I hated.

It's possible they sense my unbelief, my lack of faith in anything. It's possible they can't bear that. When I ran over the field where the frenzied women had strewn your dismembered limbs, when I ran over that field, wailing in the deepening darkness, and gathered you up, poor, broken brother, piece by piece, bone by bone, that's when I stopped believing. How could we be meant to come back to this earth in a new form. Why should a dead man's limbs, scattered over a field, make that field fertile. Why should the gods, who demand from us continual proofs of gratitude and submission, let us die in order to send us back to earth again. Your death opened my eyes wide, Apsyrtus. For the first time I found solace in the fact that I don't have to live forever. And then I was able to let go of that belief born out of fear; to be more exact, it repelled me.

I've never met anyone I could talk about this with. I found someone here who believes as little as I do—Akamas—but he's on the other side. We know a lot about each other. I say to him, with my eyes only, that I see through his deeply ingrained indifference, which excepts only his own person; he says to me, with his eyes only, that he finds my deeply ingrained compulsion to meddle in other people's affairs comical and immature. And, of late, dangerous. He warns me, only with his eyes, but I feign complete ignorance. I want to know now.

I went away with Jason because I couldn't stay in that lost, corrupt Colchis. It was a flight. And now I've seen on the face of King Creon of Corinth the same scowl of arrogance and fear that our father, Aeëtes, showed in the end. Our father couldn't look me in the eye at the funeral rites held for you, his sacrificed son. This King here feels no pangs of conscience, if he bases his power on a heinous crime, he looks everyone brazenly in the face. Since Akamas took me with him across the river and into the necropolis, where the rich and distinguished Corinthians are interred in gorgeously furnished burial chambers; since I've seen what is interred with them so that they can get through the journey into the realm of the dead, and no doubt also so that they can buy their way in, gold, jewelry, food, even horses, sometimes servants as well; since then, I can see this whole glorious Corinth only as the fleeting reflection of that eternal necropolis, and it seems to me that they reign here too, the dead. Or what reigns is the fear of death. And I ask myself whether I shouldn't have stayed in Colchis.

But now Colchis is catching up with me. I threw your bones, brother, into the sea. Into our Black Sea that we loved, and that you, I feel certain, would have chosen as your grave. Within sight of the Colchian ships that were pursuing us, and before the eyes of our father, Aeëtes, I stood on the *Argo* and threw you piece by piece into the sea. Then Aeëtes ordered the Colchian fleet to turn aside, and for the last time I saw his familiar face, petrified by horror. My Argonauts, too, felt their blood run cold as they watched that scene: a woman, howling like a savage, who took the dead man's bones she'd been carrying and threw them against the wind into the sea. I musn't be surprised, Jason claims, if that scene is coming back to them now and making them uncertain what they should think, so that they don't want to appear as witnesses in my behalf. So all of you think I would have been capable, I asked him, of killing my own brother, dismembering him, and taking him with me on the voyage in a goatskin bag? He turned away, my dear Jason. He still owes me an answer.

All through these years, brother, I've been unable to dream of you. But now my memories have awoken, and with them my dreams. Night after night the foaming sea surges high once again, night after night, once again, it swallows up what's left of you, night after night I finally shed the tears I have owed you since then. And night after night my fingertips touch the delicate bones I found in that cave under the palace, the thin skull, the childish shoulder blade, the brittle spine. Iphinoe. She's more your sister than I could ever be. When I awake in tears, I don't know if I've wept for you, brother, or for her.

I know that the Argonauts tried to talk Jason into handing me over to Father. My rash flight had hung the Colchian fleet around their necks. They were on the verge of throwing me overboard so that the pursuers, my Colchians, would stop and fish me out. Jason stood his ground. He told them I was under his protection. That was new to me, being under a man's protection. He was confused and uncertain. His people began to talk about expiation for blood-guilt. It would be of help to us, they said, were we to do something to placate the gods for Apsyrtus's death, and were we to include in this expiation both my flight from Colchis and Jason's helping me to flee. I fought against this suggestion, which concealed an admission of guilt, but I saw how urgently Jason wanted to perform this act of expiation. Just then we were near the island where Circe, my mother's sister, had lived for many years. Lyssa remembered her and reminded me, and at once I, too, remembered a wild bush of red hair, and I thought, well, after all, why not, why not lay eyes once again on this relative whose fame as a sorceress had penetrated far beyond her island. The Argonauts had heard of her too, and they refused to go with Jason and me because, they said, Circe cast spells on men and turned them into swine. They steered into a hidden cove and put us off.

We met the woman on the shore, she was washing her flaming-red hair and her white garments in the sea, we looked into her craggy, fearful face; she seemed to know who was coming there, and as we were walking toward the cluster of timber houses in the interior of the island where she dwelt with a company of women, she said she'd been expecting us. She said she'd dreamt last night of streams of blood that washed over everything, including her, she'd had to cleanse herself of this blood in the sea. We were silent, as befits those come to perform an act of expiation, we crouched by her hearth and daubed our faces with ashes in your memory, brother. Circe bound the white priestess's fillet around her forehead and took the staff in her hand; then she wanted to know what bloody deed we had to expiate, and I said, My brother's death. Apsyrtus, Circe said in a toneless voice. I nodded. Unhappy woman, she said. I was overcome by an unappeasable grief, which is now starting awake again, just as my memory is being torn open and all these scraps of remembrance exposed at once, the same way new stones are thrust to the surface of a field every year.

Circe sprinkled us with the blood of a freshly slaughtered piglet while muttering the adage, Blood shall cleanse blood-guilt. She had us drink from various cups. Thereupon Jason fell asleep, but I became wide awake. We had two hours. The time seemed endless, Circe said so many things to me after I told her why I'd had to leave Colchis. She gave me the feeling that she was my forerunner and I her successor, for she, too, had been driven away when she and her women spoke out seriously against the King and his royal household, they stirred up the people against Circe, laid upon her the blame for crimes they themselves had committed, and managed to impute to her the reputation of a sorceress while undermining all confidence in her, so that there was nothing, absolutely nothing, that she could do anymore. She performed her last healing—another thing I didn't know, brother—on you and Mother, you had nearly smothered at birth because Mother hadn't enough strength to push you out of her. So Circe reached inside her with her thin, powerful hands, turned you around so that your head would come forth first, and drew you out, and then for an entire night, using all the remedies she knew (she repeated them to me), she tried to stanch Eidyia's blood. Mother's will to live had been nearly extinguished, but Circe laid you, a tiny bundle, on Mother's breast, and screamed at her that if she bled to death this child would die. After a little while the bleeding stopped. The thought of your death, brother, moved her when all Colchis had given her up for dead.

Circe knew more about the world than we did. She didn't have to budge from her island, people came to her, ships owing allegiance to the rulers of many lands sailed over that part of the Mediterranean, stories about Circe were told in the port taverns on every coast. Do you know what they're looking for, Medea? she asked me. They're looking for a woman who'll tell them that they're not guilty of anything; that the gods, whom they worship by chance, compel them in their undertakings. That the track of blood they leave behind is proper to their male nature as the gods have determined it. Great, dreadful children, Medea. And this sort of thing is on the increase, believe me. It's gaining ground. Even your young man there, the one you've got yourself attached to, even he will soon be clinging to you. The evil is already growing in him. But none of them can tolerate desperation, they've trained us to despair, because someone must grieve, either he or she. If the earth were filled with nothing but battle-noise and howling and the whimpering of the fallen, then it would simply stand still, don't you think?

How could I have forgotten all that for so long. It comes back to me only now, I asked Circe to let me stay with her, with her and the women. In the blink of an eye I lived a lifetime at her side, on this island, bathed in this divine light. The ships came and went, men came and went, comforted, healed, or perhaps not. Circe had the same thought in the same moment. Then she said that I couldn't stay. That I was one of those who must live among these people and find out where we really stand with them, and who must try to calm that fear of themselves that makes them so wild and dangerous. Even if only with that one there, that Jason.

How could I have forgotten all that. Yes, Circe said in answer to my question, laughing, it *had* so happened that she'd chased a gang of men off the island as swine, thinking that perhaps this might help them attain a glimmering of self-knowledge. Do you know something, Medea, Circe said to me, do you know what I believe? I'll become really wicked as time goes on. Little by little I'll become wicked and do nothing but stand on the shore cursing and refuse to allow anyone else on the island. All the malice and meanness and vileness they pour over me doesn't just run off my back like water.

How could I forget that. How could I forget that I, too, wished I might become wicked at the right moment, really wicked. And now, Apsyrtus, the right moment seems to have arrived.

Unfortunately I'm only stunned. Because everything's so transparent, so easy to see through. Because that doesn't matter to them one whit. Because they can look me in the eye unflinchingly while they lie, lie, lie. Not being able to lie is a terrible hindrance. Our childhood game comes back to me, brother, the one we played in order to learn how to lie. The winner was whichever of us served up a given lie to Mother or Father so innocently that they believed it. Generally they laughed and sent us packing—neither of us was very good at that game. These people here, Apsyrtus, are masters when it comes to lying, including lying to themselves. From the very beginning I was amazed at the lumps and knots in their bodies. If I laid my hand on the back of their necks, their arms, their bellies, I felt nothing, no movement, no flowing. Nothing but hardness. I was amazed at what a long time I'd need to melt that hardness, at how unwilling they were, at what a fight they'd put up. What a fight they'd put up against sympathy. And then, how they'd sometimes dissolve in tears, mature, experienced men. And how they'd often fail to return, wouldn't let me near them, because they were ashamed. I had to learn to understand that first, and Jason was helpful to me there.

He was a gorgeous man. His gait, his posture, the play of his muscles during maneuvers on the ship—I couldn't keep my eyes off him, and when some of his Argonauts were wounded by the Colchians, Jason and I looked after them. He knew what he was doing, he, too, was familiar with the palpations, the healing remedies. I've never been closer to him than on that night, when we worked shoulder-to-shoulder and communicated with each other without using words. And so I had nothing against becoming his wife, and not only because otherwise the King of Corcyra, where we had sought refuge, would have turned me over to the second Colchian fleet, which had been ordered not to return home without me. So that very night we performed the prescribed wedding ceremonies and consummated our union in the grotto of the old Goddess Macris, under whose protection I urgently placed myself, and I laid my jewelry upon her altar. Since then I've never worn jewelry again, that was my vow to the goddess, she understood me. I gave up my rank. I was an ordinary woman, in her hands. I gave myself to Jason like that, without holding anything back, and thereby bound him to me. Yet today I remember clearly how I clutched his shoulders when he lay on me, how I could feel his every muscle, his straining, his satisfied weariness. And how woeful I was when his shoulders, too, like those of the other men of Corinth, grew stiff and hard. How he stopped suffering from that. Became a courtier. For the three of you, he said. For you and the children. So they'll let you stay here. He wasn't saying "us" anymore, he was saying "you," that was what cut me. A pain that won't go away.

King Creon can try to insult me and intimidate me, he can put on his stony face and pass me by without a word or a look. It leaves me cold. Akamas can go on and on at me about how I should stop trying to learn more about the dead man I stumbled on in the cave, because if I'd stop, the rumor that I killed my brother would fade away on its own. Then I say, What makes you think those were the remains of a man, and he turns white and clenches his teeth so hard his cheekbones protrude and he asks me menacingly, What do you know, Medea. I don't reply.

But if Jason comes to me all worried and overwrought and asks me the same question, and if he, too, tries to silence me, that won't leave me cold. I'll tell him what I know: that the bones of a young girl, almost a child—about the same age as you were, little brother—are lying in that cave. And that they're the King's daughter's bones, the elder daughter of King Creon and Queen Merope, the silent Queen, who spoke to me when I visited her in her gloomy chambers. I was only one question away from the truth, she had only to say yes or no. Her thin lips gave me the answer. He commanded it, Merope said. He wanted Iphinoe out of the way. He was afraid we'd set her in his stead. And indeed, that's what we wanted to do. We wanted to save Corinth.

The cold that pierced me then has yet to leave me. One of her rawboned maids saw me out. I wandered around the courtyards of the palace with a stone in my breast I can't get rid of. She wanted to save Corinth. We wanted to save Colchis. And the two of you—this girl Iphinoe and you, Apsyrtus—you are the victims. She's more your sister than I can ever be.

I should never have left Colchis, never have helped Jason get his Fleece. Never have persuaded my people to come with me. Never have taken it upon myself to make that long, terrible crossing, nor lived through all these years as a barbarian in Corinth, half feared, half despised. The children, yes. But what will they meet with. There's nothing else anymore but victors and victims, my dear brother, on this disc we call Earth. And I've got a craving to know what I'll find when I get driven out over the edge.

Five

Akamas

> As soon as women are made our equals, they're our superiors.
>
> CATO

Oh, blast these simpletons. It's simpletons that will drag us down to ruin. I hadn't believed it possible that this sort of thing still existed. Admittedly the rumors that went ahead of her couldn't fail to whet one's curiosity, seafarers who came ashore here had met the *Argo* as well as that woman in one or another of the ports around our great sea, all the tittle and tattle of the sailors' dives washed up on our coast. I couldn't name anything that caused more of a stir in those days than the Argonauts' adventure, nor any subject that set more jaws in motion than the woman people quickly began to call the Beautiful Savage. I know my fellowmen, I think I'm entitled to say that, I know their curious, irrepressible needs, I know their prolific imagination and their tendency to take the products of that imagination for undiluted reality, but this woman must have set off some spark that burned inside their brains and never went out.

King Creon, who's no fool when it comes to his cousins who occupy the thrones of the countries around us, foresaw pretty clearly what would happen. That the capture of the Golden Fleece wouldn't do Jason any good at all, because his usurping uncle wouldn't yield him his throne. That he wouldn't find anyone who'd help him fight for his inheritance. That he, together with his wife and her retinue, would have to seek out a safe place to take refuge in. That place, King Creon told the Council of Elders, will be Corinth. He'd never met this nephew, but he'd made inquiries about him; the reports were not unfavorable, he said. Of course, the upbringing Jason had received from Cheiron in the Thessalian forest could not be compared with the advantages that Kings' sons enjoy here with us in the palace, but nevertheless he had developed certain abilities, tamed others, cut back some unruly weeds. As for the rest, we could no doubt take care of drumming that into an able, receptive young man. We all nodded. After all, there was no male heir at this court, only a daughter, the unfortunate Glauce. The Augurs, too, having given the matter due thought, hid their eyes and murmured their assent with their mouths. As they were leaving, Creon held me back; this flattered me, but I'd have preferred it if he hadn't singled me out in front of all the others and thus aroused their envy.

What do you think, Akamas? He had grown accustomed to taking me into his confidence, and every time I had to calculate whether he wanted me to speak frankly or merely to confirm his opinion. I said a young man of Jason's stature would well become the Corinthian palace. Good, good, but what else. Then there's the matter of this woman, Creon, I said. I know, said Creon. We'll have a close look at her, right? Just so, said I. I had to make the necessary arrangements for the arrival of Jason and his people.

A few weeks later, on a windy, cloudy fall day, the *Argo* and the Colchian ships that had accompanied Medea sailed into our harbor. A pilot ship from our fleet guided them in, some palace officials of the second rank had been delegated to receive them. I stood a little to one side and waited for the woman. With Jason supporting her by an elbow, she came down onto the landing stage, stepping resolutely but heavily. She was far gone in pregnancy, pale, exhausted, hollow-eyed, the rough crossing had been too much for her, the women who attended her had been afraid she'd go into labor on that rolling, bucking ship. I saw that she was beautiful and understood Jason. Then she was standing before me, and I saw her eyes, the golden sparks in her green irises. Her eyes were lively and alert. As long as a woman's feet are cold, she said, the birth can't begin; these were the first words I ever heard her speak. The Colchians gathered around her the way chickens disturbed by a thunderstorm rally around a broody hen; they formed a dark, crouching flock on that gloomy shore, while the lowering clouds came rolling in above them. Marooned, I thought. That must never happen to us.

Jason gave me the names of the few Argonauts who were still with him and courteously expressed his gratitude for the welcome he hoped the refugees would find among us. I had to remind him that he'd forgotten to introduce his wife to me. This threw him into a terrible confusion. Medea laughed. After her eyes, it was her laugh one recognized her by. It's been a long time since I last heard that laugh, I know well that we're the ones who smothered it, unfortunately we must do quite a few things that we find personally distasteful.

That very night she was delivered of her babies, they were twins, wait, I should say they are twins, two boys, healthy and strong, one of them blond like Jason, the other dark and curly-haired like her. She had to laugh boisterously again, about that. The births weren't difficult. Several times we who were making ourselves busy in the corridor outside her chamber heard her women chatting among themselves and even singing. When the palace officials asked Lyssa about this unusual merriment, she said childbirth was a joyous occasion that people should celebrate. I don't wonder that many of our women, including some from the best families, have had the Colchian women teach them their way of giving birth, but our learned physicians forbid the Colchian healing arts to pass the threshold of the palace. And they're right to do so. The Colchian women's methods of healing aren't suitable for us. When a child is born to one of them, you'd think his sole obligation was to be here in the world, and all love and care are due him for that reason alone. Now, that may well be a good and beautiful thing, but it is of course primitive, and after all the efforts one has made to free himself from this admittedly warm but above all cramped breeding cavity, it makes no sense for him to fall back into it at the very first opportunity. Women, yes indeed. One can observe in many of them a strange desire to spend time with the foreigners, as though they've been seized by some compulsion. Then they begin giving their husbands thoughtful, detached looks. To tell the truth, I enjoy this. I'm no friend of those worthy men. As for their chilly, affected women, I'm no friend of theirs either. I've got something against such adhesive friendships. Agameda senses that. We're alike. And, in any case, soon it's going to be all over with Medea's clandestine fame as a healer. Who's going to want to consult a woman who has murdered her brother. We must do quite a few things that give us little pleasure.

In the beginning she was trusting, and that certainly had its charm. It was a curious thing for me to see my city through her eyes. Why, she might ask, why are there these two Creons. There's the stiff one in the throne room, and there's the relaxed one at table when we're by ourselves. Well, it had never entered my mind that things could be otherwise. At the time, you see, King Creon used to dine with Jason, Medea, and me, he'd be in a good mood then and he'd let himself go. Sometimes poor Glauce was with us, filled with nervous admiration for Medea. The King, her father, paid no attention to her. There's a rumor going around that Medea is treating her falling sickness, and in fact Glauce does seem to be recovering, it's a shame I'll have to put a stop to that. In answer to Medea's simpleminded question, I tried to make it clear to her that Creon, as King, is not Creon or any other man whatsoever, in fact he's not a person at all, but an office, namely the King. Whereupon she said, The poor man. Agameda told me only recently that she must have been thinking about her father then, the King of Colchis. A strange woman.

I gave way to a peculiar impulse and explained to Medea how Corinth functions, which further entailed letting her know, little by little, the various ways I exercise my power, among them making sure that it remains invisible and that everyone, especially the King, is firmly convinced that Creon, and he alone, is the source of power in Corinth. I couldn't resist the thrill of breaking through the isolation and discretion I'm condemned to and making this woman, who's not of our world, into a kind of confidante; it amused me to see that she couldn't appreciate at all the gift I was giving her, because she considered it a matter of course. That was in the days when we could still afford to play such games with foreigners. We were sure of ourselves and our city, the King's chief astronomer could allow himself the luxury of explaining to an immigrant, who could never and under no circumstances become a danger to us, what the glory and wealth of his city are based on. For everything depends on what a man really wants and what he considers useful and therefore right and good. Medea didn't argue with all of that statement, the only part she rejected was the important "therefore" in the middle. What's useful, she said, is not necessarily what's good. Gods! How she tormented me—and above all herself—with this little word "good"! She was at pains to explain to me what the people of Colchis had supposedly considered good. Good was anything that promoted the development of all living things. So, fertility, I said. That, too, said Medea, and she began to speak of certain forces that unite us humans with everything alive and that must flow freely lest life come to a standstill. I understood. Here in Corinth, too, we've got a little band of dreamers who talk like that. But seriously striving toward such an ideal, I pointed out to her, would make life in any kind of community impossible for man as he now is. She thought it over. That depends, she said. On what, Medea. Let me be, she said, it's starting to dawn on me, I don't know how to express it yet.

Talking with her is always stimulating. But I can also understand how she could get on people's nerves. Creon, for example, and it serves him right, his is not exactly a fine brain, he gets himself driven into a corner and then demands that I get him out. In the past I gave myself the pleasure of playing dumb and pretending not to hear or see his signals. The woman was too cunning, in his opinion, and too impertinent. Above all, she gave him the creeps. She was— how shall I express this—too much of a female, it even colored her thinking. She considered, but why on earth am I speaking of her in the past, she believes that thoughts develop out of feelings and should not lose their connection with them. Old-fashioned, of course, outdated. Animal dimness, I said in addition. Creative source, she replied. All night long she stood beside me in my observation tower and explained to me Colchian astronomy, which is practiced only by women and based on the phases of the moon, and had me tell her our names for the constellations, describe their courses, and recite the conclusions about our own destinies that I read in the movements of the heavenly bodies and their constellations. We listened to the music of the spheres, a crystalline sound our ears are not attuned to but which they can nevertheless perceive in rare moments of extreme concentration. Medea was the first woman to hear this note in the same moment that I did. As though a mighty bow were stroking a vibrating string, she said. That's exactly how it was. That night, I must admit, this experience shook me more strongly than usual, and in a different way.

I was offended by her unwillingness to go along with the predictions I based on my observations of the starry sky. After all, we in Corinth have an ancient astrological tradition, the list of my predecessors, whose names we reverently pass on, is long, and though I permit myself thoughts that are off the prescribed path, this in no way diminishes my desire to be added to that list one day and thus to live on in the memory of my countrymen. Why? Medea asked once again. I couldn't help noticing that her questions were bringing her closer to a field around which I'd drawn a boundary that no one was permitted to cross. I might say as well that her questions first made it plain to me that this field existed and dredged up again all the painful and embarrassing causes that had compelled me to create it for myself. At that point I became surly. Why, why! I shouted. Why does a man want to live on! The question was superfluous. She grew silent in a way that expressed her disagreement more strongly than any words could. So what is it, I began again, you don't want to live on in the memory of your people, or what? She hadn't yet given that any thought, she said. Maybe she could persuade some people of that, but not me, I said. That silence again. Something akin to fury was beginning to rise in me, an emotion I'd rid myself of because it was unworthy of my estate. Much later, in a completely different connection, she suddenly declared: In our country all ancestors are honored, you know. Sometimes I had to laugh.

Naturally my Corinthians gaped at the little troop of immigrants as though they were strange beasts, not exactly in an unfriendly way, but not exactly friendly either. We were having some good years back then, of course one only notices that afterward, we basked in the Colchians' amazement at our prosperity. Several good harvests, one after another, had filled our stores and kept food prices low, now and then there was a public feeding for the poorer classes, and our dependence on the Hittites was barely noticeable. But what seemed to me equally significant was this: the unhappy story of Iphinoe was finally forgotten, I barely remembered it myself. Nobody was asking anymore whether she had really been abducted by foreign seamen in order to enter into an honorable marriage with their young King. Furthermore, though I wouldn't have believed it possible, the people had been willing to accept that Merope, their well-beloved Queen, was permanently ill and lodging in that remote wing of the palace, and that she refused to see anyone, anyone at all, with the exception of those two unspeakable females. I myself don't even know whether she had been ordered to do so and was therefore condemned to a kind of exile, or whether after the incident with Iphinoe she was, on her own volition, avoiding everything connected with the palace like the plague. At some point I stopped inquiring into the matter.

I was young when all that happened. We were living in uneasy times, the peoples all around our Mediterranean were in movement, internal discord was threatening our city too. There were two parties in the Council, one was devoted to Creon, the other backed Queen Merope, who had an important voice, because according to an old and by now thoroughly pointless custom the King would receive the crown on loan from the Queen, and royal power was inherited through the female line. All at once these old, forgotten laws had regained significance, and the two parties were locked in a bitter struggle. A neighboring city proposed an alliance that would have made Corinth secure and immune to attack, but only under the condition that Iphinoe marry the city's young King and be named as Creon's successor. Many members of the Council, among them Merope, found this proposal reasonable and the prospect of freeing Corinth from the clutches of various great powers highly desirable. Creon was against the idea. Without or against him, nothing could be got through the Council. Merope was furious, she saw clearly that the King's refusal was directed against her. I was on Creon's side. It just doesn't make sense, he told me in a confidential moment. After a prolonged, difficult process that demanded a huge expenditure of craft, patience, and persistence, we separate Merope from any power or influence, only to fortify the hopes of a new petticoat government in our daughter Iphinoe and the women who've attached themselves to her? Not, he assured me, that he had anything against women. Indeed, the history of the peoples around our sea gave sufficient examples of successful female dynasties. What had decided him was not self-interest, only concern for Corinth's future. For whoever knew how to read the signs of the times could see that all around us, amid strife and horror, states were taking shape, and a Corinth guided by women as of yore would simply not be a match for them. And it was pointless to rebel against the current of the times. One could only try, he said, to identify it early enough to avoid being swamped by it. Of course, the price one might be called upon to pay for this could be very painful.

Our price was Iphinoe. If we hadn't sacrificed her, I told Medea, Corinth would have perished utterly. What makes you so sure, she said, it was the obvious question for her to ask. My hair had literally stood on end when this hate-consumed Agameda and this unspeakable Presbon came in with their denunciation, and when I began to realize that Medea knew everything. And that she was caught in a trap. Through her own fault, quite so, that enraged me even more. What makes me so sure, I shouted, she was asking *me* that question, when I'd lived through those events, yes, I thought I could even say *suffered* through them? She might instead consider whether it was really her place to instruct anyone as to how he should behave toward his country and its royal family. She remained strangely unmoved. As far as coming to terms with Colchis and her flight, she said, I could safely leave that up to her; but I ought to be aware that all this underhanded propaganda, knowingly based on a false accusation against her, was superfluous. She had never planned to talk about what she'd found in the cave, nor about what she'd learned. And she knew how to keep quiet, I should know that. She'd only wanted clarity for herself. But perhaps we couldn't bear even so little?

We were facing one another as enemies. I couldn't let myself feel any remorse about that. Just don't be so arrogant. Just don't be all too sure of yourself, my dear Medea, I told her. Propaganda, you call it. But when your own countrymen, with no urging from us, have become suspicious all by themselves? Do you think it so far-fetched that they might ask whether they were, perhaps, persuaded to take flight under false pretenses? Whether perhaps someone had a very personal interest in leaving the country before the fratricide became known?

I was expecting flaming rage, but all I got from her was scorn. Far-fetched? Most certainly. Extremely far-fetched, after all those years, and all too convenient for our interests. Which, incidentally, would be better served if we didn't have this excessive dread of exposure. For if it was true that without Iphinoe's murder—she said murder—Corinth's continued existence would have been threatened, then why didn't we believe our Corinthians capable of understanding that fact now, after so many years? And of having enough comprehension to value the continuation of their own lives, and lives of ease at that, above the life of a young girl. Or would we absolutely insist on further hypocrisy and further lying, and accept all the sacrifices that such a policy would necessarily entail? For I must be able to foresee that it wouldn't be pretty for anybody, including us.

She knew what she was talking about. I didn't even consider answering such questions. It couldn't have escaped her that my dear

Corinthians' lives of ease depend directly on their ability to consider themselves the most innocent people under the sun. It's really ridiculous to assume that people are improved by hearing someone tell the truth about them. They just become discouraged and stubborn when that happens, unbridled, ungovernable. In this respect I am of the conviction that it was the right course, indeed the only right course, to perform the sacrifice of Iphinoe in secret, and that those who ordered it as well as those who carried it out should be praised for it, because they took upon their own shoulders a heavy burden for us all. I was not present. It couldn't have been pretty. I certainly know how one sacrifices a young bull on the altar.

An altar had been erected in that underground gallery, and therefore it's outrageous to talk about murder. The girl, a charming child—I knew her, of course—will have been completely unsuspecting. Her mother, Merope, had to be kept under guard by four men in that part of the palace where she's lived ever since, people say her mad shrieking caused her to lose her voice and she's been dumb since then. Creon, the father, was away on a sea voyage to the Hittites, with whom he negotiated treaties that only the malicious could call acts of submission. Now, it's true, the Hittites are appealing to certain clauses originally designed to cover cases that were never supposed to occur, now they're exploiting the changes that are taking place around our Mediterranean to strengthen their hegemony. We're facing the possibility of increased dependence on them, Creon's situation is delicate, the Corinthians sense that a crisis is imminent. Medea is stirring up unrest at an unfavorable point in time, I told her that. Maybe so, she said, but she didn't see that any point in time would ever be favorable. Not for me, not for Corinth. Not for herself either. On top of everything else, she added, I'm not one of you. But you could have become one of us, said I. And she: Do you really believe that, Akamas?

No, I don't believe that.

Iphinoe's nurse went with her. This woman is supposed to have said that the child must at least see a familiar face as she died. I'm told she spoke to the girl the whole time and sang her old lullabies. I'm told she took her by the hand and led her through the torchlit gallery, walking behind the priests who had been chosen to consummate the sacrifice and in front of the royal officials charged with witnessing this consummation. Iphinoe is supposed to have asked, once, Where are we going, and the nurse patted her hand soothingly, and then just at the end, when someone grabbed her by the neck and bowed her head down onto the altar, Iphinoe asked, What are they doing. What unhappy impulse moved me to question that young official about these details? He was only too glad to be rid of them, he loaded them onto me. He said the nurse didn't let go her hand, which jerked as the knife cut deep into her throat. It is no doubt true, said the High Priest, that not even the oldest citizens of Corinth could remember a human sacrifice, and the only justification for this one is that it will spare us other and more terrible human sacrifices. The nurse, of course, lost her mind; she would run through the streets of Corinth all day long, with tangled hair and crazy eyes, surrounded by guards who didn't allow anyone to speak to her. She avoided the Queen. One day her shattered body was found at the bottom of the cliffs. The palace spread the word that she hadn't been able to get over the loss of her foster child, which was, in fact, true; like so many truths, however, this one was based on false assumptions. For Corinth had been provided with the news that young Iphinoe had eloped, and that negotiations were going forward with the royal house she meant to marry into; there was no reason for concern.

I learned a great deal from this case. I learned that no lie is too obvious for the people to believe if it accommodates their secret wish to believe it. I was convinced that the disappearance of little Iphinoe, who could walk through the streets of Corinth alone, surrounded and guarded and sustained by the people's love, by their emotion at the sight of so much tenderness and vulnerability—that Iphinoe's disappearance would cause unrest, because the deception the people had been fobbed off with was so utterly obvious. Nothing of the sort. Of course, if the Corinthians had believed the girl was still in the city, then they would have stormed any building where they thought she was being held, including the palace. The nurse's suicide had done us an invaluable service: everyone believed that Iphinoe was away. Normal people don't risk their lives for a phantom. They would rather imagine the child happily married, in a flourishing country, by the side of a young King, than dead and rotting in a dark tunnel inside their own city. That's only human. Man goes easy on himself if he can possibly arrange it, the gods have made him like that. Otherwise he wouldn't exist on this earth anymore. Songs that celebrate Iphinoe as a beautiful young bride have become popular. This brings ease to the Corinthians' hearts, it transmutes their nasty suspicions and guilty feelings into a sweet longing. One cannot be sufficiently amazed, cannot sufficiently admire the wisdom of the gods, who have set things up in this way and not otherwise. Once one sees how the process works, observing it again and again can become something of a compulsion.

I can safely say that I see how the process works. But not that I still find it stimulating. How it bores me to tears already, the thought of what will happen with Medea! How tiresome it is for me to foresee every single step of her inexorable decline. She demanded that I say publicly what I know: that she's not her brother's murderess. She still hadn't understood that an avalanche had been set in motion, and it would bury anyone who wanted to hold it back. Did I in fact want to? A curious question. I don't know the answer. Did I start the avalanche? In any case I was one of the first who saw that starting it was necessary. One doesn't always like what is necessary, but one idea has made an indelible impression on me: that in carrying out the duties of my office I have to base my decisions not on personal preferences but on more elevated points of view.

This vain booby Presbon. This Agameda, blinded by her hatred. They follow their urges without restraint. What a pleasure it would have been not just to dismiss her and her spiteful suit, but rather to have her stoned for defamation of character. If this person Agameda only knew what images I let pass before my eyes to enhance my pleasure while I'm satisfying her. But I don't live to follow my pleasure. Yes, says Medea. I know. All of you, that's your misfortune.

Was she always like this? Has she become more impudent during the time she's spent with us? Am I, because I've forgiven her so much, partly to blame for this? That's the opinion of Turon, my young confederate, who is single-mindedly positioning himself as my successor, though of course his methods are different from those that I and my generation considered permissible. These young people have no scruples, sometimes they seem to me like young wild animals, prowling through the jungle, sniffing for prey with dilated nostrils. I say such things to Turon's face. Then he grimaces as though he's got a toothache and asks most insolently whether life in our lovely city of Corinth doesn't in fact resemble a jungle. Whether I can name him a single person who's risen to the top without obeying the law of the jungle. Whether I would really advise a young man with a talent for political leadership but without either connections to the royal family or advocates in the highest circles to follow all rules, laws, and moral precepts like a good boy. Untroubled by worry or doubt, he thrusts his shiny, impertinent face at me. I have to turn away to keep from striking it.

They speak out what we scarcely think. Should we call that honesty? I spoke about this with Leukon, who was apprenticed to the King's astronomers as a very young boy, almost at the same time as I was. We meet more and more rarely, I don't go out of my way to meet him, I believe he secretly considers himself the conscience of Corinth. Honesty? said Leukon. In this case, one can't distinguish honesty from cheek. The method of people like Turon, he went on, is to take the means the old ones developed for other ends and coldly use them against us. And making sure they themselves get ahead is the only goal they have.

That was friendly on Leukon's part, the way he said "us" and included me. We both knew that I no longer belong to the group he was talking about. One can't have everything, one can't be the King's First Astronomer and remain on intimate terms with someone like Leukon.

It was, at the latest, around the time when the Iphinoe affair took place that I had to make my decision. Naturally Leukon belonged to the group of Corinthians who wouldn't stop making inquiries about Iphinoe. It seems there was a sort of conspiracy, it was crushed, I had no part in any of that. Leukon was assigned to that circle of astronomers who spend their lives observing the heavens, who perfect our maps of the stars, and who are obliged to abstain from any sort of interpretation and from politics in general. Apparently it was just what he needed; of course, the most talented people gather there, as well as the most ironical, they discuss various esoteric topics among themselves, the prevailing tone is relaxed and comradely. I naturally have no intention of letting Leukon notice when a trace of envy for his tranquil life, his commitment only to his own standards, comes over me. One can't have everything.

I might add that I came across Medea outside the door of his room in the tower. I don't like this. What's going on between them.

If she's looking for comfort from him, she's welcome to it. If they're cooking up some sort of alliance to thwart the measures that we'll have to take before long, then I won't be able to protect Leukon either anymore, but I hope it doesn't come to that. Now and then I find myself, half angry, half shocked, thinking about the question Medea asked me as she was leaving after our long talk. She asked: What in fact is it that you're all running from?

Six

Glauce

He took away my possessions.
My laughter, my tenderness, my
    capacity for joy,
my compassion, my helpfulness,
    my animality,
my radiance; every single time one
    of them appeared,
he trod it down, until it stopped
    appearing at all.
But why would someone do that, I
    don't understand . . .

INGEBORG BACHMANN,
Franza-Fragment

It's all my fault. I knew that punishment had to come, oh, I've had lots of practice in being punished, punishment rages in me long before I know its face, now I know it, and I throw myself to the ground before the altar of Helius and tear my clothes and scratch my face and plead with him to take this punishment away from my city and lay it only on me, on me, the guilty one.

The plague. Ah, that's going too far. Can there be a sin so grave it brings on a plague? I could ask Turon that, he never leaves my side anymore, Akamas has assigned him to protect me, he's my age, a pale, incredibly thin young man with hollow cheeks and long bony fingers and an oily expression, I must be thankful to him for the way he looks after me, the King is worried about me, I'm told, but governmental affairs prevent him from coming to see me personally, that goes without saying, and even if he should come I wouldn't be able to tell him that Turon's clammy bony hands repulse me, he likes putting them on my arm or on my shoulder or even on my forehead, it's to soothe me, he says, and then there's the stench of stale sweat that comes from his armpits, it nauseates me, no other person I know smells like that, on the contrary, there are persons whose smell one can't breathe in enough of, but I don't want to start think-

ing about that again, not about the woman who laid her hand on my
forehead, no, I'm supposed to forget her, I must forget her, everybody who tells me to do so is right, especially Creon, my father, he's
right, I must wipe that woman's name out of my memory, I must
drive her entire person out of my head, tear her from my heart, I
must let myself be questioned, or do my own questioning, about
how it could come to pass that I opened my heart to her, to her, who
will always be a stranger to us, Turon's probably right when he calls
her a traitress and accuses her of black magic, but actually I couldn't
care less about what Turon says, it doesn't upset me so much as
Father's desperation upset me, isn't that so, nobody has ever seen
him so angry, I can't remember that he ever touched me before, he
avoided touching me, I always understood that. What man, even if
he's her father, would want to touch a girl's pallid unclean skin, her
thin lank hair, her awkward limbs, even if she's his daughter, isn't it
so, yes, the first thing I knew for certain was that I'm ugly; the
woman whose name I don't want to say anymore can laugh at me as
much as she wants, she can teach me tricks, how I should carry
myself, how I should run, how I should wash and wear my hair,
naturally I was taken in by all that, and I would almost have believed
her, would almost have felt like any other girl; that's my weakness,
believing those who flatter me, though it wasn't actually flattery, it
was something else, something cleverer, it went deeper, it touched
the most secret spot inside me, the deepest pain, which up until then
I was able to display only to the god and will be able to display only
to the god again from now on, forever and ever, that's my sentence, I
dare not think about it, it makes me sick, she taught me that, it
makes me sick when I keep recalling to my mind those images of
myself as an unlucky person, as a poor soul, but why, she said,
laughing as only she can laugh, Turon's absolutely right, it's pretty
impudent, she's welcome to laugh that way in her wild mountains,

he says, but why should we put up with laughing so presumptuous as that—why, she said, do you want to suffocate your whole life under all this black cloth, she took off the black clothing I've worn as long as I can think, she had Arinna with her, Lyssa's daughter, who had brought some woven fabrics, the kind only the women of Colchis know how to make, colors that made my eyes open wider, she held the cloths against me, she led me to a mirror, but that's nothing for me, I said, they merely laughed, it should be a particularly bright blue, Arinna said, that will bring out your coloring, with gold borders on the neckline and the hem of the skirt. She sewed the clothes for me, both of them had to do a lot of talking before I'd wear them, I ran through the halls with downcast eyes, one of the young cooks didn't recognize me and he whistled at me after I passed, unheard-of, unheard-of and wonderful, oh how wonderful, but her black magic was just that, she let me feel something that wasn't real, isn't real, all of a sudden my arms and legs became graceful, or anyway that's how it felt, but that was all deception, ridicule, Turon says, and sympathetically lays his hand on my head, he means of course ridicule of a pathetic, unhappy wretch afflicted by the gods, and the proof of all this is that now, when they've taken me away from her corrupting influence and given me back the dark-colored clothes I belong in, that now my arms and my legs, too, have lost their deceitful gracefulness again and no apprentice cook, no matter how stupid, is even going to think about whistling at me, which would be extremely impertinent behavior toward the King's daughter, that's what Creon shouted when he finally caught on to that woman's game, after it was reported to him that she was visiting me regularly, often, What have we come to, he shouted, can anybody here do whatever they want, I throw this woman out the front door and my daughter lets her in again through the back door; Creon grabbed me by the shoulders and shook me, my father touched me, that had never yet happened, that was fear and joy at the same time. I'd pulled it off, I'd pushed him so far he touched me; she should see this, I thought, I wanted to show her, her who wanted to take away my fear of my father, that any joy I got from him would have to be mixed with fear. I should have been scared, but I wasn't scared, yes, that's it: I confess everything, I admit they're right, but I'm not scared, not of myself, not of her, but I wonder whether she actually knows that people immediately start behaving differently whenever she enters a room, that even the King, my father, would never have allowed himself such an unrestrained, yes, unrestrained fit of anger in her presence, when she's there even he holds back his true feelings, because all of a sudden they embarrass him, I was quick to notice that, just because I don't say much it doesn't mean that I don't observe things and have my own opinions about them, she told me that straight out, by the way, at our first meeting. I remember every word she said from the very beginning.

Of course, no one can imagine how I waited for her and the other Colchians, how fervently I longed for them to come, I bribed the young servant girl I had then to give me some of her old clothes and disguised myself as a girl of the people, I hid my face with a shawl and slipped through the barriers around the port, I can be very bold when I'm not Glauce. And so I was standing at the foot of the landing stage and saw her coming down with her great belly, leaning on that man whose radiance blinded me, something broke apart inside me, I saw her shape outlined against the sky, how I hate it, this Corinthian sky, I've never told anyone that, only her, always her again, her, her, yes, she was the one who wanted to teach me to hate, But please, not the sky, Glauce! she cried out, and laughed in her way, yes, she was the one who tried to persuade me that I was free to think, I hate my father, and nothing would happen to him because of that thought, there was no need for me to feel guilty about it. That's how her wicked influence on me began, today it seems incredible to me, outrageous, that I surrendered myself to it, that I reveled in my surrender to it, that was the wickedness in me, all at once it was free to present itself as my best side, my obsession with fancy dress, the pleasure I took in trivial diversions and in those childish games she made me play with Arinna, Arinna, whom she brought to me as a friend; I'd never had a friend who took me with her to the sea and taught me to swim, I got to hear about how healthy it was, and for a while it looked as though they were right about that, didn't it, even my trouble came over me less often, she claimed it would stop altogether, there were days, weeks, when I no longer awoke in fear, waiting for it to grab me and shake me and throw me thrashing to the floor, but Turon says, How can anyone deceive a sick person with such a cruel lie, he worries a great deal about me, and he's near me when it comes over me, he catches me, he holds me up, it's his responsibility to see that I don't injure myself, he calls for help, I believe the whole palace knows how often I get thrown down, I see it in their pitying and contemptuous looks, I can't take a single step alone anymore, I can't sleep alone anymore, Father's so afraid I could hurt myself in some way, or so I'm told, whereas that woman urged me to take the secret path to the sea all by myself, if they only knew, Arinna would be waiting there for me, sometimes as I drew near her in the dusk she wasn't alone, a male person was with her, a shadow-man whose silhouette I recognized, who moved away when they saw me coming, and about whom Arinna said not a single word, it was only that she was aroused, excited, she couldn't hide it, we were on familiar terms with each other, but something held me back from asking about the man, I scarcely wanted to believe that what I saw was true, but then Arinna began talking about it on her own, it was the first time a woman took me into her confidence, yes, she was quite attached to Jason, my heart jumped, I didn't let a word escape me, I was learning. And his wife? I dared to ask. She knew, I discovered. She seemed natural enough when she met the two of us together. She listened to our chatting, but in the middle of ordinary small talk she might break in, might ask what was the first event I could remember, such questions, I had to laugh at them, But people just don't know that, I'd say, Ah, she'd say—while she massaged my head and neck in a way that did me a world of good and dissolved the vibrating heaviness that stayed in the center of my head and almost never went away and sometimes seemed an awful force that blew my poor head all apart and brought on my trouble—she said I didn't have to worry about that anymore, but she'd be interested to know the first event I could remember and how I'd felt when it happened, she told me I should take my time and get my courage up and let myself climb down an inner rope—one can picture it that way, she said—to a deep place inside me that was nothing other than my past life and my memory of it. That's the way she talked, wicked as she was, always so casually, while she was setting off a chain of events without any notion of responsibility for them, Father's right about that, of course, and he was beside himself after he and Akamas had got me to reveal the lengths she'd driven me to. Inwardly driven me, I mean, for she restrained herself too, she only had me drink her herb broths, sometimes they tasted good, sometimes they were bitter as gall, and she never again mentioned that rope that for a while was more real to me than all the objects of the outer world. And me on it, going lower down, climbing down, deeper and deeper down. Not only when I was lying on my bed but also when I was walking around with my eyes open, even when I was talking to someone, at the same time I was able to, no, obliged to follow, with close attention, this smaller copy of myself that was struggling to get to the bottom in me. Sometimes I grabbed for her hand, and she let me hold onto it. She wanted to persuade me that I mustn't deny them, the shadows that so often fell over my brightest days, I mustn't run away when the terrible fear took hold of me, every time I got near a certain spot in the palace courtyard, near the well, so that I'd had to learn to avoid that spot. Sure, a person can live with that, most people haven't a clue how much avoidance a person can live with, but then it started happening not only on that one spot, then it was the whole area around the well, finally it was the whole palace courtyard that made me tremble, and I became quite inventive with excuses and pretexts that helped me get out of having to enter that courtyard, which every one of us crossed several times a day. I didn't reveal my sickness, not even to her, but she could tell anyway, from a sound I made, from a jerky movement, and I was surprised at how closely she was watching me. She'd taken me seriously when I declared, I can't! and didn't try to talk me out of my fear, I know, she said, it's just as though you'd lost an arm or a leg, except that no one can see what you're missing. She was patient, that was surely part of her plan, and I couldn't say exactly anymore how she got me to take hold of her hand one day and cross the courtyard. She held me very tight, I still remember that, she spoke to me softly as we approached the spot and my hands became damp and my feet tried to plant themselves in the ground, she soothed me with her words, no, it was more than soothing, it was one of her sorcerer's tricks, that's clear to me now, because all at once I stopped being aware of anything except a great silence, and when the sounds came back again I was at the other end of the palace courtyard, sitting beside her on the stone bench in the shade of the ancient olive tree, and so I must have run and passed that spot without going into the fits I dreaded so much, it almost seemed to me as though I should try to bring them on so that everything would be the way it was supposed to, but she said that wasn't necessary anymore, she laid my head in her lap, stroked my forehead, and spoke softly of the child I once was and of the unbearable memory associated with that spot in the courtyard that I'd had to forget in order to stay alive, which was only natural, except that as that child grew up the thing she'd forgotten grew up with her, it was a dark blotch in her head that kept getting bigger, do you understand me, Glauce, until it overcame that child, that girl; oh, I understood her, I understood her only too perfectly, she was throwing me the rope, I was supposed to lower myself down on her questions, she wanted to guide me past the dangerous spots I couldn't pass alone, she wanted to make herself indispensable, I had to see that.

It took a long time before I was obliged to admit that I had fooled myself on this point too, had let myself be fooled, but then what's right anyway, can I still trust my own eyes, can I still rely on anybody at all.

I don't know, I really don't know how she got me talking, I mean, talking about what I'd forgotten, it only came back to me the instant I told her about it. Maybe I'm making that up now, I said, That doesn't matter, she said, my head lay in her lap, I'd never laid my head in anyone's lap before, But maybe you have, she said, maybe you've sat like this with your mother and you just don't remember it anymore. What makes you say that, I cried out, she didn't answer, she never answered direct questions, that's one way of seeing how calculating she was, she figured that I wouldn't be able to stand the silence and would have to go on talking, would have to talk myself past my embarrassment, I talked and talked until I let a sentence drop that suited her purpose, it was something casual, unimportant, but she snatched it out and used it to trip me up. Was that the first time your parents quarreled? Why, I said, what do you mean? I'd just told her that one day my mother—she must have still been living with us in the palace then, still beautiful, with her long curly raven-black hair—that once she stood here in the palace courtyard and shook her fists at the sky, tearing her hair out in clumps and shrieking. I twisted my head around in that woman's lap, it always starts like that, and it would have yanked me back into the comfort of forgetting, but the woman, she wouldn't stand for that, she set her force against it, she held my body tight and said in a firm, angry voice: No! Go on, Glauce, go on, and I saw the man my mother flung herself upon, who called her by her name and tried to keep her off him, she was scratching his face with her fingernails. Who was this man, Glauce. The man, the man, which man. Be calm, Glauce, be very calm, look closely.

The man was the King. My father.

I hate her. How I hate her. I can believe she killed her little brother. She's capable of anything. If she's allowed to do it, someone like her must necessarily draw down on a city all the evils that the gods can send, she should simply disappear as though she'd never been here, she herself taught me that there's no thought I must forbid myself to have, she believes everyone is permitted to think about their most unthinkable desires, but now I wonder whether she'd have kept on believing that if she had known what all my unthinkable desires were. For that was my secret triumph and my deep anxiety, I had escaped her, I and my hidden longing; she, who seemed to know more about me than I did myself, she didn't suspect how far my desires, set free from fear by her, went beyond their proper bounds, nor what shape they took, nor what shape they were attached to. Nor what voice, for it was his voice that I heard first as I was waking up from a kind of deep sleep, with my trusting head still lolling in her treacherous lap.

She's coming to, said a gentle, anxious male voice, my gaze fell on the handsome face that was bent over me and on two indescribably blue eyes. Jason. I saw him as if for the first time, I listened to the sound of his voice as he and the woman fretted about my welfare, I have no words to express what my feelings were then, I stood up, I felt better and worse at the same time, it simply wasn't possible to focus my longing on the man who belonged to that woman, and it simply wasn't possible to stop doing so. She said to me, You've tried for so many years to reconcile irreconcilable things that it's made you sick. After that wild fight with my father that I'd witnessed as a little child, my beautiful mother withdrew from me, it was as though she avoided all contact with me whatsoever. Soon I was covered all over by a skin rash that itched and tormented me, and then Mother came again and fixed me compresses of milk and curds, and she sang songs to me that were coming back to me now, but was she showing me her true face or not, hadn't she always preferred the other one to me?

What other one, the woman asked me, naturally, we talked continuously wherever we met, not in the palace courtyard anymore, hardly ever in my room, she seemed to be avoiding the palace, she employed Arinna to carry messages to me, but these couldn't give the impression that they came from her, again and again she got me to tell her everything that was going through my head, all random and confused, just as it came, and I noticed that my thoughts were turning more and more frequently to my mother, who had abandoned me and about whom I didn't want to know anything more. Maybe you do, she said, maybe you do want to know something about her after all. Do you realize why she lives in her gloomy chambers and doesn't open her door to a single soul? That, I said, is something I don't want to know, Turon claims she's not completely right in the head, and I believe that, I can even see it, I watched her at the banquet, sitting at the table like a mummy next to my father, you could feel sorry for him with such a Queen, and then she didn't even look at me, didn't even turn her head in my direction, to say nothing of asking about me, but left, simply went away, and my trouble came over me again, Yes, I said to the woman angrily, she wished it on me, every time I see her or talk about her, it comes over me. That may have been the case, the woman said, but it's not the case any longer.

It was incredible, but she seemed practically delighted when I broke out in that hideous skin rash again, I was beside myself when it started, first in skin folds, then it spread over big areas of my body, disgusting, oozing, and itchy, It's a sign of healing, she asserted, and what was it you said? Milk and curds? She fixed me the same compresses as my mother and hummed my mother's songs to boot, she gave me one of her nastiest tinctures to drink, she showed me the places on my body where the rash was in retreat and new skin was appearing, Glauce, she said cheerfully, you're sloughing your skin like a snake. She spoke of rebirth. Those were days filled with hope, until she deserted me, just as my mother deserted me once, that's something she should never have dared to do. I hate her.

Now, I'll bet, her arrogance is fading. It's being said, louder and louder, that she killed her little brother, and today I heard voices that named her name in the same breath with the plague that has claimed its first victims down in the poorer quarters of the city; Agameda, who's sweet enough to look after me, mentioned this rumor in passing, it seemed to me she was watching my reaction to it very carefully. I had my face under control, but triumph and horror nearly took my breath away. Now she would get what she deserved. They're preparing to make some move against her. They're keeping it secret from me, but I can get all the information I need to know, I put on a silly expression and ask the servants naive questions, they're so used to considering me foolish, or more likely stupid, that they speak quite openly in front of me. If you're scared, you must be well informed about your surroundings, like a weak animal in the jungle, the woman understood that precisely, she knew precisely how fear resists attempts to drive it out, how close it lurks below the surface, waiting to burst out again, she tried, I admit, as long as she could, to maintain contact with me, even when she herself had good reason to be scared too.

One day Arinna, playing innocent as usual in such cases, asked me whether I might like to see one of the city's best sculptors and stonemasons, Oistros, at work. I'd heard a lot about him, he makes gravestones for high-ranking people, it's said that the gods gave him golden hands, but what I noticed first were his eyes, gray-blue, penetrating eyes, friendly, yes, but not only friendly, searching as well, I found in them no trace of that prying, pushy, envious quality that I find in the eyes of most Corinthians. Ah, he said, Glauce, it's good of you to come. He has rust-red hair, that's unusual in Corinth and regarded as a blemish, but not by Oistros, mockery and slander bounce off of him. He showed me around his workshop and explained the different kinds of stones and what he uses them for, he demonstrated for me how he applies the chisel, he pointed out blocks of stone and had me figure out what shapes are hidden inside them—for it's not true that just any shape whatsoever is hiding inside any stone, that was new to me—it's the same way with us, Oistros said, you can't make a human being out of every mass of flesh, sometimes it's comforting to know that, don't you think? He treated me as his equal, he laughed loud and infectiously, and as he was laughing two women's heads appeared in the doorway of the next room. I was startled. She, that woman, was here. The other one I didn't know. Oh yes, said Oistros, I believe you're expected, and he pushed me into the next room.

I had never imagined that there could be in my city anything so beautiful as that room. Arethusa, who lived here and seemed to be on quite intimate terms with that woman whose name I avoid saying, Arethusa was a gem cutter, her head had the same profile as the jewels that she cut out of their stones, her dark curly hair was piled elaborately on top of her head, she wore a dress that emphasized her narrow waistline and left much of her breasts bare, I couldn't take my eyes off her. Why haven't I ever seen you, I asked without thinking. Arethusa smiled. I believe, she said, we move in different circles, I work a great deal and seldom go out. Her room was filled with exotic plants, there was a great opening in the wall facing west, you hardly knew whether you were inside or outside. This would be a good place, I thought, and I felt a tightening around my heart because places like that, where life is good, aren't granted to the likes of me, but now I have to think about all of that in the past tense, the house where Arethusa and Oistros lived is supposed to have sustained heavy damage in the earthquake, I wouldn't know who I could ask about them. Another earthquake has taken place in my vicinity, a convulsion that destroyed no houses but made people disappear. It's as though the earth has swallowed up all the people who were connected with that baneful person, I would have to find that sinister if it hadn't happened for my own good, and what should I talk to Oistros and Arethusa about now besides that woman's fate, I can feel in my bones that she's heading for a catastrophe, and I fear that and long for it at the same time. Let it come, let it finally come.

This, as I well know, is the sole feeling that Jason and I share. Jason, who has lately been turning up in my company more and more often, and every time my heart skips a beat, it's too dumb to care that Father sends him to me. Jason's bound to someone else and always will be, I know that for certain, no one can ever get free of her. But can someone like me refuse a gift sent by the gods, must I not gather up the crumbs that fall to me from another's table, they taste bitter, but also sweet, sweeter and sweeter the farther away he is, because then he's with me in my mind, speaks with me as he has never spoken with me, touches me as he will never touch me, gives me a happiness I've never known, ah, Jason.

The woman will be destroyed, and that's all to the good. Jason will stay. Corinth will have a new King. And I shall take my place by that King's side and I'll forget, forget, finally I'll be able to forget again. Which she wouldn't allow me to do, that woman, I feel ill when I think about how she tormented me. There was a certain afternoon at Arethusa's when five of us—Oistros had joined us, and also, to my astonishment, Leukon, who was said to know more about the stars than anyone else in Corinth and of whom I'd always been in awe—were sitting outdoors in the inner courtyard with its beautiful flagstones, some of Oistros's sculptures stood around us as though keeping watch, an orange tree shaded us, we were drinking a marvelous drink that Arethusa had prepared, I felt transported into another world, my shyness had vanished, I was joining in the conversation, asking questions. I learned that Arethusa had come here from Crete, that she and several others had been able to save themselves on the last ship to leave their island before a tidal wave struck it, it seems she was very young at the time, hardly more than a child, and yet she brought with her to Corinth many Cretan customs, including ways of preparing various dishes and drinks and the art of gem cutting, but most of all herself, Leukon said, softly stroking her arm, and she took his hand and rested it against her cheek. It was as though scales had fallen from my eyes: I was with two pairs of lovers. For even though Oistros and the woman whose name I don't mention seldom touched, they couldn't stop looking at each other. I could hardly believe it; Jason was free.

So we sat and talked and drank and ate the tasty meat patties that Arethusa brought out, the afternoon heat gradually abated, the light faded, the others went away one by one. I was alone with the woman. She walked a few steps with me to a rivulet of water that was flowing out of the basin of a fountain. We sat down on a patch of grass, I must have said something about the beautiful afternoon, about my pining for such days, they come so rarely, I must have opened my heart to her once more, and she managed again to lead me into those depths where the images of the past lie buried. Into that abyss, where I saw myself, still a small child, sitting on the stone threshold between one of the rooms of the palace and the long, ice-cold corridor and weeping inconsolably. What kind of room was that whose threshold I was sitting on, she wanted to know, but I didn't want to look around, I was afraid, she whispered that soothing patter of hers, then I had to turn around. It was a room where a young girl lived. There was a chest painted in gorgeous colors, clothes were spread out on the bed, a little mirror framed in gold stood on a console, but there was no sign to indicate who might live there. You know who, Glauce, said the woman, you know exactly. No, I cried, no, I screamed, I don't know, how should I know, she disappeared completely, was never seen again, nobody ever mentioned her again, even the room disappeared, I probably made it all up, she probably never existed at all. But who, Glauce, the woman asked. My sister, I screamed. Iphinoe.

Iphinoe. I had never heard that name again, never spoken it again, I could swear I'd never even thought it, not since that time, and why should I, she was gone away, my older sister, the beautiful one, the intelligent one, the one my mother loved more than me. She disappeared between one day and the next, on that ship, Turon says, ogling me with his close-set eyes, along with that youth, he says, and moves quite close to me, I can smell his sour breath, with that son of a mighty but quite distant King, she'd simply fallen in love with the young man, says Turon, the power of Love, don't you know, you've felt it too, and as he says this he twists the corners of his mouth in a disagreeable way, and then he says, so it happened that she went aboard the ship in too much of a hurry, Iphinoe, carried off in the gray light of dawn, without telling me good-bye.

I act as though I believe him, but he doesn't know everything, the stupid Turon, for she did indeed tell me good-bye, my sister did, in the gray light of dawn. I told the woman this too, on that mild evening in Arethusa's inner courtyard, trusting as I was, it was easy to speak in the dark, easier than ever before, easier than ever again. Some noise in the corridor had startled me out of sleep, I went to the door and looked out, I said, and now I saw before me the image I'd forgotten for so long, my sister, thin, pale, wearing a white dress, in the middle of a troop of men, armed men, that surprised me, two in front of her, two who had her between them and were holding her there by the arms, or maybe they were just supporting her, and close behind them came our nurse, with such a face as I'd never seen on her before, it scared me, I said to the woman, who seized my hand and held it tight, but I noticed that her hand was trembling too. And then, I said, when they were a few steps past me, then my sister turned around and smiled. She smiled the way I'd always wished she might smile at me, I said, I believe she really noticed me for the first time, I wanted to run after her, but something told me I shouldn't do that, they moved away quickly, very quickly, and turned a corner, I could still hear the armed men's steps echoing, then nothing more. Then my mother's shriek. Like an animal that's being slaughtered, I'm hearing it again, I said, weeping. I wept and wept and couldn't stop, she, the woman, held my shoulders tight, they were shaking as in a fever, she said nothing, I saw that she was weeping too. Later she told me that the worst was now behind me. Is Iphinoe dead, I asked. She nodded. I'd known it the whole time.

But what does "known" mean? We're capable of letting ourselves be talked into believing a great many things, aren't we? Turon's quite right about that. She, this person, wanted to make me fall under her sway, as women of her type do by nature. She was the one who filled my brain with all these images, all these feelings, that's no trick for her with those potions of hers, which they've naturally taken away from me. She built up all kinds of groundless suspicions in my mind, that sounds believable enough. Or would you rather believe, my dear Glauce, that you live in a murderers' den? asks Turon, making that grimace he thinks is a smile. That our beautiful Corinth, which these foreigners can never understand, is a kind of slaughterhouse? No. I don't want to believe that. Of course I imagined the whole thing. How could a child, as I then was, be capable of taking in such complicated images and keeping them locked inside herself for years and years? Forget it, says Turon. Forget it, says Father, better times are coming for you now, wait till you see what I've got planned for you, you're going to like it. That's how he talks to me now, my father. Ah me.

What's the matter outside there, what's going on. What's the meaning of this sound, louder and louder, coming from so many throats. What are they shouting, what's this accursed name to me. They want her. Gods! They want the woman. Helius, help.

It's coming again, I can feel it, it's already strangling me, it's already shaking me, is no one there, will no one help me, will no one catch me, Medea.

Seven

Leukon

People want to convince
themselves that their misfortunes
come from one single responsible
person who can easily be got rid of.
  RENÉ GIRARD, *Violence and the Sacred*

The plague spreads apace. Medea is lost. She's fading away. She's fading away before my eyes, and I cannot hold her back. I see plainly what will happen to her. I shall have to stand by and watch the whole thing. That is my lot, to have to stand by and watch everything, to see through everything, and to be able to do nothing, as though I had no hands. Whoever uses his hands must dip them in blood, whether he wants to or not. I do not want to have blood on my hands. I want to stand up here on the roof terrace of my tower, observing the milling throngs below me in the narrow streets of Corinth by day and bathing my eyes in the darkness of the heavens above me by night, while one by one the constellations emerge like familiar friends.

And if these fickle gods should yet grant me one wish, the names of two women occur to me for whom I would beg protection. I am surprised at myself; a woman's name has never played a part in my life before. Not that I have abstained from the joys that the eternal play between man and woman can bring, but the names of the girls who visited me, whether once or oftener—they were always quite willing, by the way, even delighted—their names quickly passed out of my mind, their visits became rarer, and I found that I did not miss them very much. Medea says that I am a man who fears pain. I should like her to fear pain more than she does.

She is still sitting across from me on the terrace, a bit of air is moving after the insufferably hot day, we begin to breathe more freely. A little oil lamp stands between us on the low pine table, its flame is almost still. We drink cool wine, speak softly or remain silent. We have not given up this habit of our nightly meeting, although other people generally creep into their burrows and avoid one another. An uncanny stillness lies over the city. Only now and then one hears the noise of the donkey carts carrying away the day's corpses, taking them across the river, whose black shape lies there below us, and into the necropolis. I count the carts. Their number has increased in the last few nights. Medea is lost.

What will become of us, Leukon, she says, and I do not have the heart to tell her what I know, what I see is to become of her. She arrives, glowing with beauty and flushed with love, from Oistros's house, she embraces me, and I embrace a woman who is no longer there. She does what she should not do, she tosses my warnings to the winds, and there is no talking to Oistros at all. With his chisel, which is the extension of his fingertips, he frees the image of the goddess from the stone and does not even seem to notice whose likeness he is reproducing. Medea is in his fingertips, she has taken possession of him, he says so himself, nothing like this has ever happened to him, he says, the lust he feels for this woman has given him a new lust for life and for his work. When I draw near his house I can hear him in his workshop, whistling and singing; only when she enters does everything become quiet. The man has no parents or relatives, knows nothing of his origins, and seems neither concerned by this lack nor weighed down by his fate, which was to be abandoned as an infant and laid before the door of a stonemason, whose childless wife welcomed the foundling as a gift from the gods and raised him as her own; while still a child in his foster father's workshop he learned the fundamentals of his craft, soon growing beyond them, as the old stonemason candidly and almost reverently would admit. These days the very noblest Corinthians commission him to make the gravestones for their families. He could be a rich man; no one really knows how he manages to remain so frugal and modest, nor understands why he has not aroused the envy of the other stonemasons. Money seems to cling to him as little as envy does, but in compensation he amasses people. He's always surrounded by young admirers, whom he puts to work in his shop. His carefree nature attracted me too; when I was with him, I was cured of my melancholy brooding, which he seemed not to notice—in any case, he never spoke a word about it. And this was precisely what was salutary about his presence, he treated everyone the same, and I am sure he would not make a fuss even if the King himself were to wander through his door. And, curious to observe, his equanimity and independence are communicated to all who visit him, whether high or low.

Medea says he has succeeded in becoming an adult without killing the child in himself. He was a blessing to her, but is he still? I should not ask such questions. I would certainly refuse to tolerate it if anyone should ask me whether I consider Arethusa a blessing, despite the renunciation she imposes upon me. We have tacitly agreed to keep our relationship, though it is no such thing, a secret, while of late Medea visits Oistros virtually without taking precautions. Her carelessness is becoming dangerous, indeed criminal.

It drives me to despair. As though someone wished to revenge himself upon me for keeping my feelings in check for so long, the people I must lose my heart to, of all the people in Corinth, are those who do not really know how things stand here and have no idea what the Corinthians are capable of when they feel threatened, as they do now. Medea drinks, smiles, falls silent. Akamas has already taken me to task about my friends; we met, apparently by chance, on the steps of the tower, at the twilight hour—he had chosen the time and place well. You seem to prefer precisely those people who have placed themselves at a rather considerable distance—thus did he express himself, my slyboots Akamas—at a rather considerable distance from our ruling family, haven't you, my dear Leukon? And I, more and more frequently overcome these days by helpless rage, did not answer his question, but instead asked a few of my own. Was there any breach of duty he could accuse me of? Was he not perhaps trying to make me responsible for the dubious conclusions others had drawn from my meticulously correct calculations? Akamas yielded the point, but we both knew I could not enjoy my victory. I dared not permit myself too often to rub Akamas's nose in his hair-raisingly false predictions, as though I did not know who had read into my star maps what the King wanted to hear: a happy year for Corinth, growth, prosperity, and the defeat of the King's enemies. Instead of which came an earthquake, followed by the plague. Akamas's star was on the wane at court, he was declining before our eyes. He cannot live if he is not foremost in the King's favor, once he told me this to my face, at the time when a young girl was sacrificed on the altar of power in our proud Corinth and those who knew of it had to decide whether they wished to bask in that power or to withdraw from it.

You knew about that, Medea says in the tone of one making an observation, and I try to explain to her that knowledge is like a ladder. Up to a certain rung, yes, I knew, but no details. And then I forgot it again. What else could we have done, I ask her. She says she doesn't know. But it's just a shame. A shame? I ask. Yes. A shame that agreements are so breakable and could simply be shoved aside at the least pressure. What agreements, I ask. But you know what I mean. The agreement that there is to be no more human sacrifice. I am amazed that she takes such agreements seriously, but I say nothing. Today I do not like the way she is talking, I do not like her mood, it is as though she were moving behind a veil.

I must rouse her from her sleep. I tell her that Akamas is dangerous now, that he will do anything to reinforce his position in the palace. Since I am of use to him, I am temporarily safe. What I do not tell her is that I must summon up all my practical knowledge, all my intelligence, all my cunning, in order to secure my safety, and that I moreover need to exercise a talent she detests in me—I myself do not love it—a talent for keeping silent and ducking out of the way. At well-thought-out intervals I deliver to Akamas calculations from which he can make favorable predictions, which in their turn come true; concerning, for example, the conclusion of a trade agreement with Mycenae or higher birthrates among our livestock. I make sure Akamas can be convinced that he and no one else has made these predictions, perhaps they have appeared to him in a dream; I must hide my own light under a bushel so that his star may shine all the more brightly. The stars in the galaxy of Creon's court have arranged themselves anew, to the detriment of the little planets, which find themselves pushed into the dangerous marginal zones. And it is a fact plain as day that the situation is growing increasingly dangerous for anyone who exposes himself to the reflection of the light that emanates from Medea. She, yes she, is the danger's very center. And here is the awful thing: she will not admit it.

I don't know what still has to happen, I say to her, before you start being more careful, and she has the nerve to reply that precisely because so much has happened to her, perhaps now she can count on being left in peace. She is keeping very still, she says, what else can she possibly do. This woman is missing something that all we Corinthians suck in with our mother's milk. We never even notice it anymore, only comparison with the Colchians, and especially with Medea, made me hit upon it. Call it a sixth sense, a fine nose for detecting the tiniest changes in the atmosphere surrounding the powerful, upon whom we, every single one of us, depend for life or death. A kind of constant terror, I say to her. So that the real terror, the earthquake, seemed to many a liberation. You are strange people, she says, and I reply, So are you. We laugh.

I do not wish to tell her that the confidence she exudes is called arrogance by most Corinthians and they hate her for it. I have given no other living person so much thought as I have this woman, but it is not just her, the other Colchian women give me a great deal to think about too. They perform the most menial work here and hold their heads as high as do the wives of our highest officials, and the strangest part is that they cannot conceive of themselves as acting in any other way. This pleases me greatly, and it disturbs me at the same time. Around you, I say to Medea, I always have mixed feelings. Oh Leukon, says she, you use your thoughts to take your feelings prisoner. Why not simply let them go? Then we laugh again, and I wish I could forget her plight, could give my feelings free rein and simply enjoy being the friend of a woman who is more familiar to me than almost any other person and who will always remain a stranger to me.

Like Arethusa, but that is a different matter. The strangeness of the beloved adds to her charm, which has, incidentally, not escaped the notice of other men either. They all realize that I have succumbed to her, even Akamas condescended to make a patronizing remark about my good fortune in love. He was quite near to clapping me on the shoulder, man-to-man, and the look I gave him only just managed to hold him off. So they must all know about us, their jaws are hard at work on the subject of me and the passion that has overtaken me at long last. This is not to be borne. If they knew that I must share Arethusa with the old man, the one everybody just calls the Cretan and a good many take for her father. He is her oldest love-friend, or so she calls him. She was hardly more than a child when he picked or rather pulled her out from under the ruins of her house, which, like all the houses on Crete, including the palaces, whose splendor must have been unequaled, was destroyed by the seaquake. All Crete must be a rubble heap and a corpse field, I know that only from the old man's accounts, Arethusa never talks about it. Likewise she never talks about the crossing they made, nor the ship on which the old Cretan, then a man in the prime of life, secured places for both of them. By force, as I once coaxed him to admit. Sometimes it happens that he drinks himself senseless, and then he talks more than usual, but never in Arethusa's presence. I have no wish to imagine the scenes that took place at this ship's departure.

The old Cretan is still a powerful man, though prematurely aged and marked before his time. He was one of the athletes who used to perform so brilliantly in his homeland, in the presence of the royal family and the assembled people, as part of the annual festival productions held in the royal palace and renowned all around the Mediterranean coast. Arethusa is devoted to him, that is an incontrovertible fact of nature. The only choice I have is to accept it or to make a clean break with her. Neither is possible for me. I never knew that life holds this kind of pain in store for us, and Medea is the only person I can talk to on this subject. She has not the slightest inclination, incidentally, to feel sorry for me. Yes, she says, I know this situation is giving you a hard time, but just imagine, nothing that could give you such a hard time might ever have happened! And you're learning to know yourself, aren't you, through what you're doing. I am not doing a thing, I say, attempting to contradict her. I merely wait. But she will not accept this. Waiting is doing something too, she says, it has to be preceded by a decision, namely, that one is going to wait and not break off. Besides, she goes on, I do indeed seek out Arethusa's company, make no secret of my feelings and my desires, and hang around her workshop hour after hour, watching her hands as she cuts the gems from their stones. No one can imagine how those hands speak to me. Arethusa smiles, she never sends me away, her face always lights up when she sees me standing in the doorway; she hugs me close by way of greeting. Do you understand that, Medea, I ask. Yes, she replies. Arethusa loves two men, each in a different way. And you? I ask, seeking to provoke her, but she retains her composure: Not I. She embraces Arethusa—they love each other like sisters—pulls the door curtain aside, and goes to Oistros.

Akamas's view of the matter is perfectly just: I have fallen among people who will not let themselves be dragged into the gears that turn the Corinthian cosmos. Sand has got into the works, they rattle and grind; this does not seem to bother them, but it makes me uneasy. I cannot criticize Arethusa on this account, I cannot criticize her on any account, but it does happen that I secretly reproach Medea for so dispassionately contemplating the signs that point to the ruination of Corinth, clearest among them the efforts to get rid of Medea. Shall all my years of practice in self-effacement have been in vain? Shall my attachment to this unloved city never cease?

Our thoughts seem to have reached similar points by separate ways. Medea asks whether it has ever struck me that a small kernel of good lies buried inside every evil. For how, without this outbreak of the people's wrath against her, should she have met Oistros, or I Arethusa? How, had she not been persecuted, should she have wandered into that remote part of the city, into that quarter with its tiny clay huts nestled in their gardens, where the poorest Corinthians have set up residence, former captives and their families as well as shady characters of every kind, among whom such people as Oistros, Arethusa, and the Cretan are not conspicuous.

It was a bright, transparent day in early summer, it was the hour when the light turns into darkness almost without transition, but not before summoning up one last effort of brightness that can still swell my heart though I have been accustomed to it since my childhood. These are the moments when I am grateful that I live here and cannot imagine living anywhere else, and it was with this precise feeling that I was standing on the tower platform from which I have gazed into the heavens on so many nights, abandoned to the unearthly beauty of the stars in their courses, whose hidden laws I wished to trace; that was my life. Indeed, I am not yet old, at least so Arethusa says, but things had reached the point where my only remaining friends were stars, not people anymore. I maintained then, as I do now, a courteous distance between myself and the young people who study under me. Now and again one of them has demonstrated high aptitude and a thirst for knowledge, as opposed to the usual ruthless interest in his own advancement shown by the single-minded Turon, one of the cleverest of them, and one of the most unscrupulous.

On that afternoon one of my pupils came rushing up the stairs, even though they all know that in such hours of contemplation I am not to be disturbed. He called out: They're chasing Medea through the city! I asked, Who? but I knew the answer already. The mob. It had to happen like this.

I dashed down the steps and without ceremony barged into Akamas's workroom, his big room with its many windows and the terrace running around it. I said: You must be satisfied now. At first he tried to play dumb, but I—and I myself can hardly believe this anymore—moved toward him so menacingly that he backed up to the wall and protested that there was nothing he could do, she had outraged the people too deeply. The people? I said, and thereupon he tried in all seriousness to serve me up the fratricide story, which indeed had been cooked up in this very room and put into circulation from here. Ah, I said with a sneer, these people all by themselves came up with the idea of starting a riot, waylaying the woman, and chasing her through the streets in disgrace, is that right? That's the way it must have been, Akamas dared assert to my face; I know only too well that no one person can stand against an angry mob. You have to let it wear itself out. Wear itself out? I shouted. Do you mean wear the woman out, or what? They're going to beat her to death! But no, said Akamas, not at all. Such rabble are too cowardly. Nothing will happen to her, you'll see.

I was, finally, beside myself. I shouted that he, he himself, had incited the rioters and quite possibly paid them off as well. Then I became scared. Of course I was right, both of us knew that, but I had gone too far. Akamas felt it too; he drew himself up, approached me with measured steps, and said coolly: You'll have to show me proof of that, my friend. He had won. I would never find a witness who would testify that the great Akamas had bribed a mob to attack a woman. And if by chance there might be someone mad enough to do so, he would be a dead man. During those few minutes, while I mentally went over all the possibilities of convicting Akamas and had to reject them one by one—it was during those minutes that I got to know my Corinth for the first time. And I grasped the fact that it had fallen to Medea to lay bare the buried truth that determines our communal life, and that we would not tolerate this truth. And that I am powerless.

I do not like thinking about that afternoon, I do not like talking to Medea about it, although I can to this day relive in my mind the long battle of words I fought with Akamas. Even though I could not call him to account publicly, I could make him pay by showing him that I had seen through him. That I knew why this particular time had been chosen to proceed against Medea, first with hair-raising accusations and then with violence: because now there was cause to

fear that she could bring to light a name we all wanted to forget—
Iphinoe. It was a relief to me to speak this name to Akamas for the
first time, to tell him that as a young person in those days I had sat in
his antechamber and heard many things I did not at first understand,
and when at last I understood them, when all the bizarre single
elements finally came together in my mind to form an image that
made my blood run cold, by then it was too late. What kind of city
do we live in, I asked Akamas angrily. His only reply was a look that
said, You know very well what kind. I described the scene to Medea;
I confessed to her that my boldness had evaporated, that a feeling of
futility paralyzed me, that I held my tongue, left Akamas standing
there, and ran off in search of her, not knowing whether cleverness
or cowardice had the upper hand in me. In circumstances like that,
Leukon, she said, it's often impossible to tell.

We fell silent. While they were chasing me through the city,
she said, I was afraid, and I ran for my life just as any hunted beast
would have run, but a part of me remained cold, deadly calm, because something was happening that had to happen. A soft voice
inside me said, It could be worse. Is it a comfort to think that people
everywhere fall short of the agreements they have made? That taking flight can't help you anymore? That conscience no longer has
any significance when the same words, the same deeds, can mean
either rescue or betrayal? There are no more foundations that conscience can build on, I learned that once as I was gathering up my
little brother's bones from the field, and then again when I touched
the girl's fragile skeleton in that cave of yours. The thought of making my discovery public never occurred to me. I just wanted to be
clear in my own mind about what sort of place I was living in. You
sit in your tower and gather the vault of heaven around you, Leukon,
that's a fortified position, isn't it? I understand you, ever since I came
here I've watched the corners of your mouth droop lower and lower.

I'm worse off, or better, depending on your point of view. It's come to the point where there's no more pattern for my way of being in the world, or maybe none has yet been made, who knows. I ran through the streets, everyone got out of my way, all doors slammed shut in my face, my strength was giving out, I found myself in the outlying parts of the city. The narrow paths, the squat clay hovels. I rounded the corner of a house with a lead on my pursuers, and there was a man standing in the way, a powerful man with disheveled red hair who didn't get out of the way, who stood his ground and caught me up and hauled me the few steps to his door and carried me inside. The rest you know. Since then I have a place in this city once again.

Not long afterward, the earthquake struck. It lasted only a few seconds; its center lay in the southern part of the city, where the poorest people live, including the Colchians. My tower swayed but did not collapse. I can still feel in my limbs the indescribable sensation you have when you lose the ground under your feet. I ran outdoors, the streets were filling with people screaming, and the end of the world seemed near, though it had not been in the stars. Damage to the palace was limited; the walls had not collapsed, though a few of the servants were injured and one killed. But King Creon's self-love, his feeling of personal immortality, had been gravely wounded by the idea that his precious life could be snuffed out by any common stone that happened to fall on his head. A grudge against everybody began to mount in him. Since then the fear of death must have never left him; he became irritable and dangerous, and Akamas in particular bore the brunt of the new, harsher tone the King adopted. I cannot rid myself of the suspicion that it was Akamas who, as a diversionary measure, once again poisoned the minds of the people, this time with the suggestion that Medea could have conjured up the earthquake in Corinth through her evil arts. I asked Medea whether she knew this. She nodded.

Once I had the opportunity to talk to Lyssa about her. It was on the evening of the earthquake, which had surprised Medea while she was at Oistros's house. I found her there after a run through the rubble to see if Arethusa was safe. Arethusa was unconscious, overcome by fear when the quaking too vividly recalled to her mind the disastrous destruction of Crete. Medea brought her back to consciousness, rubbed some invigorating ointment into her forehead, and then left her with me. She felt compelled to go to her people in the wrecked part of the city; she asked me to go and see about Lyssa and the children. The little hut was still clinging to the palace wall. I stepped out of the wounded, groaning city and into a place of rest. Lyssa was serving the children a simple evening meal, to which she invited me. I noticed how hungry I was and how much good the calmness she emanated was doing me. She is one of those women who would give the earth a kick if it should ever come to a standstill; she holds the lives of whoever is entrusted to her firmly in her hands, and one can only envy children so lucky as to grow up in her care.

Lyssa had kept her worry about Medea hidden from the children. They were carefree, full of life. The one who resembles Jason is a strapping lad, bigger than his darker, curly-haired brother, who in his turn is more boisterous and unruly. They outdid each other in their stories about the earthquake, which had been an adventure as far as they were concerned. Then suddenly they became tired and went to bed. All at once the hut was filled with a deep stillness. Lyssa and I sat in the tiny kitchen, the fire still glowed on the hearth, the house snake rustled among the ashes; we felt the relief that comes after a great danger has passed. What the next day would bring did not yet concern us. We sat in silence, then spoke in half-sentences whatever was going through our minds. We talked about Medea too, and it turned out that we had reached similar conclusions, though our points of departure were different. Lyssa saw, as I did, that a kind of malady has befallen Corinth, a disease hardly anyone is willing to get to the bottom of. Lyssa was afraid that sooner or later this would take a self-destructive turn—she was familiar with the process—and then all those demonic forces that an ordered community knows how to keep under restraint would be unleashed; and then Medea would be lost. This was the first time that I spoke to a foreigner about the state of things in our city, so now I went further and asked her what she saw as the cause of our imminent ruin. She found the question easy to answer. Your sense of your own superiority, she said. You consider yourselves superior to everyone and everything, and that distorts your vision; you don't see what really is, nor do you see yourselves as you really are. She was right, and her words are still echoing in my mind today.

The consequences of the earthquake were far worse than the quake itself. The royal household was concerned only with its own members. A high-ranking court official, killed by falling debris, was buried with great pomp; this display of lugubrious splendor showed the wretched Presbon, who had lost all self-control, at the height of his talents, but also revealed his paltriness and lack of scruples, for even he should have known that such wastefulness must arouse the wrath of the Corinthians who had lost all their worldly possessions and whose dead were in many cases left to rot for weeks under the rubble of their houses. Medea's warnings naturally fell on deaf ears, but even the physicians around Creon cautioned that these corpses had to be dug out of the ruins and buried, for they knew from experience that the dead posed a danger to the living. In fact, the first cases of the epidemic appeared in the immediate vicinity of that devastated quarter where the survivors were living in makeshift accommodations, together with the rats and in close proximity to the dead.

The hairs on the back of my neck stood up straight when Akamas had me summoned and confided to me the state secret: the city was in the grip of the plague. Trembling, I asked Akamas what he and the King were planning to do. Whereupon his thin lips moved and he spoke as though giving me the most obvious answer in the world: We're leaving the city. Steps had been taken, he said, to nip in the bud any outbreaks of panic. The security forces had been reinforced. And then Akamas pronounced a sentence that I have not yet been able to repeat to Medea. He said: And your Medea would be well advised to get out of Corinth too.

I understood him at once. I know this way of thinking, I was brought up with it, I, too, can do it. I stammered, But you wouldn't. I was superstitious, afraid of putting my suspicions into words. But Akamas understood me anyway, and he said drily: Why not.

The plague is spreading. Medea has done more than anyone else in these last weeks—the sick call for her, she goes to them. But many Corinthians claim that she drags the disease along in her wake. They say it was she who brought the plague upon the city.

It cannot be that she does not hear these voices. Cautiously, obliquely, I talk about the human need to lay one's own burden on someone else. Soon one prisoner out of every hundred will be sacrificed in order to satisfy the gods and persuade them to withdraw their chastising hands from our city. This won't do any good, says Medea. And also, she won't allow it. I start to feel cold. Urgently I beseech her not to do anything against the laws of Corinth. I'd be glad if I didn't have to, she says tersely. Medea, I say, if they don't sacrifice the prisoners, they'll look for another victim. I know, says she. I say, Do you also know how cruel people can be? Yes, she says. But we all have but one life, I say.

Who knows, says she.

I stare at her. What do I know about this woman, what do I know about what she believes. I should like to ask her whether there is any faith that frees its adherents from the fear of death, which so obsesses us. I look at her in the growing light of dawn and do not ask her. For the first time I think that perhaps she has a secret that is hidden from me. What I cling to is the conviction that we cannot escape the law that rules us as it rules the movements of the stars. Whatever we do or fail to do can change nothing in that regard. She firmly opposes this idea. That will destroy her. You can do whatever you want, Medea, I tell her, nothing will do you any good, not until the end of time. What drives men on is stronger than any reason.

She is silent.

The night is fading, and we are still sitting there. The sun comes up, the roofs of the city sparkle and glisten. We shall never sit together like this again. Now I understand what it means to say, I have a heavy heart. I see no way out that would not be disastrous. I have said what I could say. What has happened cannot be undone. What shall happen was decided long ago, without us.

We shake the rest of the wine out of our glasses against the sun and do not tell each other what we have wished for. I have not wished for anything. I think a mechanism has been set in motion that no one can stop anymore. Fatigue weighs down my arms. Should I wish that Medea would become as tired as I am.

She says, Well, I'm going. Go, I say. I stand at the parapet and watch her as she crosses the square that surrounds the tower and that is as empty as all the rest of the city. Swept empty by fear of the plague.

Eight

Medea

The festival has lost all of its ritual
characteristics, and it ends badly
insofar as it finds its way back to
its violent beginnings. It is no
longer a hindrance to the forces of
evil, but their ally.

RENÉ GIRARD, *Violence and the Sacred*

I'm waiting. I'm sitting in the windowless chamber they showed me into and waiting. A glimmer of light comes through the door, and two guards stand in front of it with their backs turned. And in the great hall they're sitting in judgment on me.

Now everything is clear. They mean me. Lyssa says I shouldn't have dared go to their sacrificial rites, that was pure arrogance. I didn't contradict her again the way I did on that morning, when was it, yesterday, the day before yesterday, three days ago, when I awoke early, looking forward to accepting the invitation from the Priestesses of Artemis and attending the Corinthians' great spring festival as a foreign guest. Was that arrogance? I don't know, it was rather something like confidence that I felt that morning. The power of reconciliation. An outstretched hand, I thought, why should they spurn it. Today I know why. Because they can calm their fear only by raging against other people.

It was a beautiful morning. A dream that dissolved as I woke up had opened a floodgate, a sense of well-being washed over me, without any reason, but that's always the way it is. I threw back the sheepskin I've slept under since I left Colchis, jumped out of bed, felt the shock of the cold clay floor under my feet. Luxuriously I put one foot in front of the other, stretched out my arms, turned around and around, and then moved into the pool of pale early morning light that fell into the room through the door. Up there in the dark, night-blue sky, like a slightly tilted sliver of peel, the crescent moon was still swimming, though on the wane, reminding me of my waning years, my Colchian moon, endowed with the power to pull the sun up over the edge of the earth every morning. And every morning the anxiety about whether the weights are still right, whether during the night their harmony has not been disturbed or their prescribed courses just slightly displaced, thus sending the earth into one of those periods of violence and terror that the old stories tell about. For this day, however, the good laws that link one star's course to all the others still seemed valid, and I watched joyfully as daylight gradually filled the nocturnal horizon. This day, in any case, would be like the one before and the one after, even my Leukon's meticulous instruments wouldn't be able to measure the tiny increment by which the arc the sun describes over Corinth would approach the vertex it will reach at the summer solstice.

By then I won't be here anymore. Neither Helius, the sun god, nor my beloved moon goddess will notice my absence. Slowly, arduously, but permanently, I've rid myself of the belief that our human destinies are bound up with the movements of the planets and the stars, that souls similar to ours dwell there and affect our lives, perhaps by malevolently tangling the threads they dangle from. Akamas, the King's First Astronomer, thinks the way I do, I've known that ever since we first exchanged glances at a sacrificial ceremony. If it's the case that both of us are dissembling, we nevertheless do it for different reasons and in different ways. He shams the most zealous of all the gods' servants because he's abysmally indifferent to everyone; I avoid the rituals as often as I can, but if I have to participate in them I keep silent, out of compassion for us mortals, who if we let go of our gods find ourselves alone, crossing a region of horrors not everyone finds a way out of. Akamas thinks he knows me, but his self-inflicted blindness prevents him from knowing anybody, himself least of all. Now he wants to gloat over my fear. I have to keep my fear in check. I dare not stop thinking.

On that morning whose details have become so precious, I heard Lyssa in the next room, blowing on the embers of the fire, then the crackling flames taking hold of the olive branches she'd stacked so carefully. Then I heard how she moved the pot of water to the hearth and began kneading the dough for the barley cakes, making it soft and supple with strokes that sounded like claps. Walking on the reed mats that she'd woven—they felt good under my feet—I went to the chest that held my things, among them the white dress I used to wear on the high festival days in Colchis. Lyssa had brought it along when we left, but recently I'd scarcely worn it. I took it out, shook the wrinkles out of it, felt it. Perhaps the material had become a bit thinner in the course of the years, but the dress was still in good condition, not threadbare. I had to laugh as I stood there naked on the mat, examining myself first with my eyes, then with my hands, my flesh no longer young but still firm, it bloomed under Oistros's hands, not slender anymore, heavier in the hips, I had to lift my breasts with my hands, but my skin had kept its lovely dark brown color, my wrists and ankles had stayed slim—ankles like a nanny goat, Oistros says—and my hair was as curly and voluminous as ever. Only a few weeks before, I'd been able to pull it out of my scalp in handfuls, clumps of hair floated in the ass's milk Lyssa used to wash it with, we both knew there was no help against the grief that had brought me a high fever and made my hair fall out. I still couldn't talk about it. It was a life-ache that concerned not only me, and not only poor Iphinoe, whose bones in the cave had started it throbbing—it was a feeling that spread inside me and grew deeper, darker, intensified by Agameda's hatred, Presbon's treachery, and Akamas's unscrupulousness, for all three together had incited the dull-witted mob against me. The turning point came when they were driving me through the streets. Suddenly I knew that I wanted to live. And then Oistros. Oistros is a powerful reason for living. This isn't the first time I've experienced rebirth through love, even my hair is clinging tightly to my scalp again. They could drag me through the city by my hair.

After plunging my face and arms into a basin full of spring water, I slipped on the dress, made sure its loose folds were falling as they should, bound back my hair with my white priestess's fillet, as was proper on a festival day, and went over to Lyssa, who was standing with her back to me, baking the first batch of barley cakes on the hearth. They released the spicy, slightly burned aroma that used to be a sign of the holy days to us at home. The spring festival was beginning for the men and women from Colchis too, but here our traditions, even when we follow them punctiliously, perhaps all too punctiliously, produce only a pale reflection of the festive mood which gave them a new birth every year in Colchis. And yet this pale reflection is better than nothing, or so most people feel, and I don't meddle with their feelings.

Lyssa turned around, saw me in my festival clothes, gave a start. Wanted to know if I was going out today dressed like that. Yes. But where? To the Corinthians' Festival of Artemis. Lyssa made no reply. I looked at her more closely, she had become older, rounder, and firmer at the same time. Of course, she's the one who keeps every detail of our sometimes complicated rituals carefully stored in her memory, passes them on to the younger people, and unshakably insists that they be followed to the letter. Never could she approve of a Colchian woman, and least of all me, who would attend a great Corinthian festival celebration, never would she acknowledge my

reason for doing so, nor agree that a conciliatory attitude could bene-
fit us Colchians. She said bitterly that my efforts to estrange myself
from the Colchians were all in vain, the Corinthians would never
thank me for making them. She was right, and I was wrong. But if I
had to do it over, I'd still have to do the same thing again. And I'd
wind up here again, in this miserable room where the air is getting
scarce, separated from everybody, from Lyssa and my Colchians,
from Oistros and Arethusa, from the Corinthians, who are sitting in
judgment on me, and even from Jason and our children. It had to
happen like this.

The aroma of the fresh cakes pulled my two boys into the
room, like foals smelling hay, I said, and they immediately teamed
up with Lyssa, What do you mean, hay? they shouted, we were
having fun again, playing the roles we'd played so often before, the
three of them against me, our voices were quarreling but our eyes
were laughing. Then the boys noticed my getup, stopped talking,
started circling me, touched the fabric of my dress, clicked their
tongues admiringly. This did me good; how long could these children's admiration for their mother last?

Then they broke apart the first barley cakes, stuffed them into
their mouths, all of a sudden I was ravenous too, I began to eat, and
as I ate I looked around the kitchen, taking in every detail as though
for the last time, every utensil, the crockery, the pots on the wall
shelf, the splintery wooden table, Lyssa's familiar shape, and especially the children, so unalike they seem not to have come from the
same mother. Meidos is the bigger one, blond, blue-eyed, the one
Jason has always especially delighted in addressing as "my son," the
one he goes riding with for hours in the countryside, the one he
hasn't made to feel any of the alienation that has spread between
himself and me. And I avoid clouding the child's bright admiration
for his father, I keep this pain reined in tight. Then there's Pheres,

my little one, round and solid as a little brown nut, woolly-haired, dark-eyed, smelling of grass, throwing himself into the act of eating as he does into every other activity, every game, with the same composed expression on his face that I love so much, with the sudden changes of light and shadow on his features, with his capacity for passing from gravity to high spirits in the blink of an eye, for weeping inconsolably and laughing hysterically. Both of them assailed me at once, I must take them with me. I had to make up an excuse; I didn't want them on my hands at the Corinthians' festival.

Perhaps it's a merciful stroke of fate that a feeling of elation comes over us when we're standing at the edge of the abyss. That morning I felt as though every burden had been lifted from me, my children were healthy and cheerful and devoted to me, Lyssa was someone who would never leave me, the walls of that modest hut contained something like happiness, a word that hadn't entered my mind for many years. Perhaps those people who are patient and know how to wait are eventually granted a profit for every loss, a joy for every pain, thoughts like this were going through my mind as I, together with the many Corinthians who were also going to the sacrifice, climbed up the steep road that leads to the Temple of Artemis.

But what's all this. What's compelling me, precisely here, precisely now, to try to reconstruct that morning piece by piece, when it seems as though it happened ages ago. I just looked through the doorway and saw all of them filing past me, heard steps coming closer. The guards in front of my door, embarrassed young men ludicrously armed with spears, could have blocked my view of those who were approaching, but they didn't. I saw them all. King Creon with his pinched face, mantled in his judge's cloak, surrounded by his personal bodyguards and followed by the Elders, who are charged with pronouncing judgments. The witnesses, among them the High Priest of Artemis, as well as the hapless Presbon, naturally, who had been responsible for the smooth and trouble-free running of the festival that I'm supposed to have disrupted. And then, among the few women, Agameda. She was the only one to cast a glance into my cell, an arrogant, triumphant, hate-filled glance. She could watch me being hacked to pieces before her eyes, her hatred would never let her go. Last of all came Jason and Glauce, my heart leapt in my breast. He had wrapped his hand around her upper arm, and he was leading her. She looked pale and strained. Both were staring fixedly straight ahead, both were pressing their lips together tightly. What a couple. Hey, Jason, I'd have liked to call out with what was left of my earlier exuberance, what have you got yourself into? So what people say about him is true, he's going to take poor Glauce as his wife and rule over Corinth after Creon's death. They had to get rid of me, they didn't have a choice.

I felt a great calm as I ascended the path to the goddess's shrine. I had to do it, that always makes me calm, even now, although this calm is more like paralysis. The beautiful, cruel city of Corinth. I became aware of it once again, for the last time, something in me said, or am I imagining that now. I was hurrying among people in festive dress, many of them knew me, a few greeted me, most looked away, I didn't care. Many were wearing signs of mourning on their clothing, the plague had spared very few families, its abatement had been announced by the palace as a propaganda measure. The higher we mounted, the more clearly we could see the landscape around the city, with its spring-green colors that would soon fade away, and we saw the carts bringing the last night's dead to the river and the shallops transporting them to the necropolis. Nobody wanted to pay any attention to these cartloads of corpses. The gold gleaming from the towers of Corinth seemed like an apparition of death to me, and a herd of twenty bullocks, earmarked for sacrifice, were being driven up the mountain by another path; we could clearly hear their fearful bellowing, and it struck me as an omen of disaster. The closer we came to the precincts of the temple, the more my morning feeling of well-being vanished away, the despondency that was weighing down this procession descended upon me too. Weren't we all victims, victims schooled in silent endurance and trotting to the slaughter. I said to myself, I am Medea, the sorceress, if you all will have it so. The wild woman, the foreigner. You shall not belittle me.

And yet. Now, sitting and waiting on the bench in this little chamber, which already seems like the dungeon it could change into at any moment, I wonder whether this conclusion could have been avoided. Whether it's really the case that a chain of circumstances I was powerless to alter has driven me to my place on this bench, or whether perhaps something inside of me I didn't have control of has forced me to go in this direction. It's futile to think about that now. But I must admit I'd find it easier to bear annihilation if it were caused by external forces. Easier, harder—words from a previous life.

Oistros and my dear Arethusa, who now has been struck down by the disease as well and whom I've been forced to abandon, and I, the three of us, used to examine all the aspects of our experiences in Corinth during our long nocturnal conversations. We talked about how this city is predisposed to undergo sudden transformations, how its brilliant, radiant, seductive character can turn into something dark, dangerous, deadly. How this ever-present danger forces the people of the city to take countermeasures against it, to wear public masks that hide their muffled, pent-up rage. Which, as we've seen, sometimes erupts. Oistros broke into my brooding about this and asked if it was up to me to placate the Corinthians. Do you know the only thing that would have helped you? he went on. If you had made yourself invisible like us, like Arethusa and me. Live in seclusion, don't say a word, don't make a face—then they'll tolerate you. Or forget you, which is the best that could happen. But this course isn't open to you.

He's right. What can they still be discussing. Is it possible they don't all have the same opinion. Is there some opposition. But from whom. Could it be that my dear Jason is screwing up his courage and opposing their judgment? But why should he do that. To make up for something? Probably not. One of the guards brings me a beaker of water. I drink greedily. How thirsty I am. How I search the young man's features for a trace of compassion. I don't find any. He's doing what he's been instructed to do. I don't find any revulsion in his face either, just indifference. After the excesses that marked the sacrificial rites, the Corinthians have regained their equilibrium. On that morning, in the long procession to the shrine of Artemis, I sensed that some disastrous violence was gathering intensity in the throng of people and venting itself in squabbles, in jostling matches at the edge of the road, and even more in the grim silence most of them were observing, in their stiff movements and their cold, distorted, tight-lipped faces. I smelled the scent of fear, which hung like a cloud over the procession, I began to feel the hard fist that was pressing against my stomach, it's pressing now too, I go on in spite of it, as I've practiced doing since my childhood, I close my eyes and see myself always walking along the banks of the same river, it's like our river Phasis, with gently sloping banks, with lush plants, with human faces turned toward me, and the pressure of the fist slowly recedes. Once when I recommended this exercise to Glauce, after a short while she burst into tears because she couldn't rid her mind of the illusion that she was walking down the long, barren, desolate path that goes toward the necropolis. I wasn't able to help her any further, my healing powers abandoned me.

Many people in the procession were carrying modest sacrificial offerings, after the drought of the last two years provisions in the city were nearly exhausted, scarcely anyone had more to lay before the goddess than a sheaf of ears of corn, a branch of olives, a couple of dried figs, no one was leading along a little goat as in previous years. The twenty bullocks, which had reached the summit ahead of us and had been driven immediately to the sacrificial altar, would provide many in the crowd with their first meat in weeks. I was hungry too, and I caught myself thinking that later I'd secretly put aside some of the sacrificed meat to bring to my sons. Behind me, I heard two Corinthians saying that the bullocks for the sacrifice had been fed from the secret store of provisions that the palace had laid in. One of the two claimed to know where the hiding place was, and this seemed to terrify the other one, because he implored his companion not to betray anything to anyone at all, especially not to him. Anyone in possession of this secret without authorization, he said, is as good as dead. Could be, the other said brazenly, but before they grabbed him he'd tell the world how the folks in the palace were living during this period of great want, his sister's son was one of the assistant cooks in the royal household, he knew what he was talking about. Just as he was about to inflict still more details upon his mortally frightened friend, his words were cut off by the gruesome bellowing of the bullocks, which made our blood run cold in our veins. The well-practiced priests of the sacrifice had cut all their throats at once.

I have heard many terrible things, but I have never heard any sound so terrible, so immense, as the bellowing of these sacrificed creatures, it was as if they were screaming out all our misery and pain in an accusation that mounted to the heavens. Our procession came to an abrupt halt. When silence returned, we began in haste to move again, forward, upward, until we could see, rising high over the temple wall, the image of the Goddess Artemis. It was a sight that made the Corinthians tremble, as well it might. A cry arose and swelled in volume: Great is Artemis, Goddess of the Corinthians. I did not join in the cry, and this caused offense. A tightly packed group of old women had been pressing closer and closer to me for some time, and one of them hissed at me, asking whether I considered myself too good to praise their goddess. No, I said, but the grandam wasn't interested in my reply, and a violent movement of the crowd separated us. An uneasy feeling came over me, but the idea of turning around and going back didn't cross my mind. And why didn't it, I wonder.

Agameda believes that not answering hatred with hatred is a form of arrogance, a way of exalting oneself above the level of ordinary people, who need hate as much as—or, rather, more than—they need love. She doesn't say this sort of thing to me, of course, we've been avoiding each other's company for a long time, but I've got informants, women who diligently relate to me everything she puts into circulation on my account. I ran into her once again at the festival. When the celebrations had gone out of control, when they had metamorphosed into a seething cauldron of violence, suddenly she was standing in front of me in the altar yard, and she flung at me a single word: Monster.

Certain individual words have always had a way of clinging to me with great persistence. Right now she, Agameda, is probably standing before the Elders and describing me in this one word, the one they've been waiting for, the one they'll pounce on gratefully. As far as they're concerned, nothing better could happen than that a Colchian woman would say about me exactly what they've been thinking for a long time. And I couldn't even accuse her, Agameda, of falseness. She really feels that the tales she's circulating about me are true, she's not touched by so much as the shadow of a doubt. I said this to Oistros, who has a profound aversion to Agameda, and he became furious. I shouldn't always try to imagine how other people feel, he said harshly.

I believe we both knew that I was sitting in a trap. Lyssa knew it too. She dismissed me that morning with an angry, tear-stained face, she wouldn't let me say good-bye to the children. I'm sure she let Arinna know what was going on. Arinna, who's been missing for weeks, and who, according to rumor, has gone up into the mountains with a small group of women. All of a sudden she was standing there, gaunt-looking, burned dark brown by the sun, her hair wild. She demanded that I go with her. She wanted to rescue me. I felt a strong urge to follow her, in the space of a few moments there passed before my eyes the life that I'd lead then, a hard life filled with privations, but free, and under the care of Arinna and the other young women. It won't work, Arinna, I said to her, and she: Why not. I couldn't explain it to her. Come to your senses, Medea! Arinna said insistently. No one had ever spoken to me like that. It won't work, I said again. Arinna raised her shoulders in despair, turned around, and went.

Now I'm tired, I've hardly slept. The awful night of the festival has got itself into my bones. The day had passed smoothly, the goddess had been offered, with great ceremony, the choicest parts of the sacrificial animals, the bullocks' testicles had been fastened to her image in three overlapping rows. I saw that Agameda was the only Colchian to have mingled successfully with the Corinthian girls whose office was to cleanse the testicles and affix them to the goddess's image, which they would then bear through the city streets as a promise of lasting fertility. While the bullocks' horns were being secured to the walls of the temple and a fire kindled on the sacrificial mound to roast the victims' flesh, the people passed the time with dancing, singing, and clowning. Presbon had prepared some festival productions the likes of which had never been seen in Corinth, he was sending out over the festival grounds waves of costumed performers meant to recall to the Corinthians' memories the glorious deeds of the past, he was stoking a mood that turned into rage when, shortly before dark, two breathless men came rushing up from the city, members of the watch, as one could tell from their clothing. They brought the news that a group of prisoners, using weapons that had been smuggled in to them, had broken out of their dungeon and, taking advantage of the empty streets, forced their way into some of the richest graves over in the necropolis and plundered them. After a deadly silence, a howl that had been awaiting its opportunity for a long time burst out among the revelers. Then what had to happen happened. The crowd began searching for victims to slake their thirst for revenge. They swayed irresolutely here and there, I thought with horror about the few Colchian women who had followed me to the festival, but they weren't the ones the Corinthians went for. They remembered the prisoners who had come to the temple seeking sanctuary from the tyranny of their masters and performed menial tasks there, that was enough of that, they should atone for the misdeeds of the others. I rushed to the doorway of the temple, implored the frightened priestesses, for the most part quite young girls from the better families, not to let this happen, to bar the temple doors and brace a wooden beam against them. They obeyed me because no one else was there to give them orders, the crowd hammered against the doors, I crept out of the temple through the secret passage behind the altar and tried to make people listen to me. I said that it was forbidden to desecrate the goddess's holy day, I shouted into their wide-open mouths, their hate-distorted faces, I thought that only through a fear greater than their rage could I overcome their thirst for blood; then an old man with a weathered, craggy face approached me and shook his fists at me. The ancestors had brought the goddess human sacrifices, he said, they were greatly to her liking, why shouldn't the people go back to the old ways. The crowd bellowed its agreement, I had lost. They began insulting me, crowding in on me, let them do it, I thought, if it has to be, then let it be now, let it be here. They had already broken through the great doors of the temple, the priestesses had fled, the frightened prisoners were crouching near the altar, many hands clutched at them. I had been pushed into the temple along with the crowd, they pressed me forward so that all at once I was standing face-to-face with the ringleader, a coarse fellow who was ostentatiously rejoicing. What do you have to say now, he bellowed, and I said quietly: Take only one. Only one, he bellowed, why should we. I said, Even your ancestors would present only one chosen human victim to the goddess as a sacrifice, more would be a gross sacrilege, murder in the temple is punished most severely. They seemed astonished, hesitated, began to confer in whispers. The old man who had first spoken to me was to decide, he gave himself a few airs, at last he nodded. They pulled a man out of the pack of prisoners, he defended himself furiously, he screamed and pleaded, appealed to his right to find refuge in the temple, he was a great hulking person with a shaved skull and a dense, curly beard, I'll never be able to forget his face, his bloodshot eyes that were turned on me. They dragged him to the altar, I didn't turn away, I saw the coarse fellow cut his throat. The blood, human blood, ran down into the altar gutters.

I have him on my conscience. Something had happened that could never be made good again, and I had played my part in it. I had rescued the others, that meant nothing to me. Why had I fled from Colchis. It had seemed to me unbearable to be given the choice between two evils. I was a fool. Now I could only choose between two crimes.

I don't know how I reached the temple court or how I came to the statue of Artemis. The first things I noticed were the sacrificed bullocks' testicles, which had been fastened to the goddess so that it seemed as though her breasts had multiplied over her entire body. Revolting ornaments, the testes of bulls, and they stank. I spat on them. If they were going to cut my throat too, these refined Corinthians, this was the right moment, I was ready. But I still didn't know them at all. Now they were avoiding me like a leper. An invisible hand had drawn a circle around me which none of them stepped across. I don't know how long I stood there at the foot of the statue of Artemis, they were in a murderous frenzy, I was deadly sober. Lyssa, who'd followed me and stayed near me without my knowing, told me later that I was a fearsome sight. Darkness was falling, the roasted bulls' flesh was cut off the skewers, torn into pieces, they tussled with one another over it, they snatched it out of the children's hands, if pieces were still bloody they devoured them raw. The outer layer has been tamed, but the bloodthirsty heart beats just under the surface. I shiver at the thought. I'm in their hands.

I felt a hundred pairs of eyes leering at me out of the flickering half-darkness, I withdrew from the circle around the fire, they did nothing to stop me. I stumbled over underbrush, vomited, stumbled some more, downhill, crossed a grove of olive trees, finally I couldn't see their fire anymore, couldn't hear their raucous bawling. The full moon was my companion. I fell to the ground in a hollow, perhaps I slept, perhaps I lost consciousness. When I awoke, a combat was going on in the night sky just over my head, a dark monstrosity was struggling with the moon, it had already taken a big, greedy bite out of her and was returning to the attack. There was to be no end to my terror.

Our moon goddess was blotted out of the sky on the selfsame night when she was at her fullest, her most comforting, her most powerful. An unknown horror seized us Colchians, penetrated our very bowels, made us fear that the end of the world was at hand. It was a deeper horror than the Corinthians felt, for whom this terrifying heavenly spectacle was nothing so much as a divine punishment, but not for any fault of theirs; no, the blame lay on all those who had introduced strange gods into their city and thus enraged their own. And so as not to have to wait, quaking, for the enormities that were sure to follow hard on the annihilation of the moon, the young men from the temple district were making ready to seek out and punish those responsible for this excessive display of divine wrath.

I'll never have the chance of asking Akamas why he kept his knowledge of the imminent lunar eclipse such a strict secret, why he required those of his astronomers who knew about it to abstain, under pain of death, from announcing its coming to their fellow citizens. Did Akamas want to bring about what has now happened? Can any person be so evil?

Leukon, who had made his own calculations, couldn't keep silent, he ran to Oistros's house, figuring I'd be there too, he wanted to notify us of what was about to happen and discuss what could be done. He found Oistros battling to save Arethusa's life from the plague. Leukon learned what they had kept a secret even from me, that the old man, the Cretan, had fallen ill first, and Arethusa had insisted on taking care of him until he died. They buried him in the inner courtyard, without handing him over to the corpse-hunting commandos that were combing the city. Oistros told me that Leukon threw himself weeping upon Arethusa, he stroked her, kissed her, pleaded with her to live, to live for him, she was still able to smile, she whispered her promise to him, he took it as a love promise, she lost consciousness, he stayed by her side. He's still with her now. That night, as the moon was growing dark, Oistros ran out in search of me. Toward morning he found me. Too late.

Time is getting short.

What happened next . . . I arose from my brief sleep, became aware of the sound that had probably awakened me, and began to follow it, all the while fearfully observing the disappearance of the moon. It was a familiar sound, a music, a rhythm that went down into my blood and led me to a barely accessible place on the side of the mountain facing away from the city, where a group of Colchian women were celebrating our own spring festival, the Festival of Demeter, which begins with a run over glowing coals. I stood on the edge of the festival ground, watching from the thorny shrubbery that surrounded it. Shrieking and laughing with delight, they were holding hands and running quickly over the glowing bed of charcoal. I saw Lyssa, Arinna. My heart began beating madly, I had to be with them. I ran to the women, they made no fuss, greeted me as though they'd been expecting me, I stretched out my hands, two of the women placed me between them, I gathered myself as I'd practiced doing so often at home, then I cried out, Let's go! We ran together over the red-hot coal-bed, once again I felt the happiness of invulnerability, I screamed for joy as they did, Once again! I cried, two others grabbed my hands, we ran, and once again, and once again, the soles of my feet remained white, unblemished. In the same moment, the heavens gave us a sign. The rim of the moon peeped out again, a narrow silver sickle that quickly grew wider. We rejoiced. So we wouldn't be lost after all. I took the laurel they gave me to chew, it sent us into ecstasy, so that we saw Demeter driving exultantly through the night, we exulted with her and began our dance, the labyrinth-dance that grows ever wilder. At last we were at one with ourselves, at last I was at one with myself. Morning wasn't far off.

Then we heard the axe.

Oistros thinks he wouldn't have found us if he, too, hadn't heard the axe and followed its sound, while the premonition of disaster that had accompanied him all along the way up from Corinth grew stronger and stronger. So it was with me too. All at once, ecstasy had vanished, and likewise joy. I didn't want to believe what I was hearing. Someone was cutting down a tree in our sacred grove. The wretch was doomed. The only thing I could think to do was to start over again the song we'd just interrupted, singing loudly so as to drown out the sound of the axe blows. The women hissed at me, held my mouth closed, I saw their distorted faces, they hated me, I hated them. They raced to the grove in a pack, sweeping me along with them, past Oistros, who drew back so that they didn't notice him, he grabbed me, held me tight, I freed myself from his grasp, saw nothing, but heard. Heard the howl of the women, my Colchian women, heard a man scream like an animal, I recognized his voice. Turon, it was Turon. I knew what was happening. They were cutting off his sex. They stuck it on a skewer and bore it along before them as they surged, out of their minds and howling ceaselessly, in the direction of the city.

Now the Colchian quarter is as quiet as the grave. The punitive operation followed on that same morning. Everyone the King's soldiers could get their hands on was massacred. It's some comfort that a few women and girls were able to flee to Arinna's hideout in the mountains.

But what am I thinking. Comfort, what kind of word is that. Many other words have snuffed it out in my heart. Speechlessness lies in store for me. Turon, having survived yet another narrow escape, Turon named my name. It had to happen thus. Mine was the first face he saw when he came back to consciousness. In spite of Oistros's pleading—I must go with him, he'd hide me, I should leave the man lying there, he was beyond help in any case—and in spite of his furious commands, I approached the unconscious Turon. He lay next to one of the trees of our sacred grove, a pine, which he had felled in order to punish the Colchians, as he declared, for bringing upon Corinth first the disaster of the plague and now the ominous lunar eclipse. Needless to say, he didn't die. In the pouch I always carry were plant extracts that can stanch the flow of blood and promote the healing of wounds. I prevailed upon Oistros to fashion a kind of litter out of two small tree trunks and some branches, and then to help me carry Turon down into the city. The gray of dawn was turning into the red of sunrise when we reached what seemed like a fortress under siege. Guards stood on every corner, armed troops were moving through the city toward the outlying districts. A young officer allowed himself to be talked into sending two soldiers to the palace with the litter. As for us, oddly enough, he let us go unmolested. We parted in the marketplace. There was no embracing. Oistros laid his hand heavily on my shoulder, he didn't even invite me to go with him. He'd understood that I had to go to the children. I haven't seen him since. I know nothing about Arethusa.

Our hut was spared by the punitive expedition, I've learned that Jason had something to do with that. Lyssa hadn't stayed with the howling women, she'd run home to the children. I'll never forget that. She remained silent.

As silent as I was when they came and put me under arrest. They charged me with having led the women who committed violence upon Turon. I made no reply. Everything was proceeding according to a plan over which I no longer had any influence. Early this morning they came and fetched me. For the trial, they said, and brought me here to this tiny dark room.

They're still discussing my case. I hear footsteps coming down the corridor. A man's footsteps, weary and shuffling. They come closer, an old man drags himself past my door, looks at the guards, then me, comes to a halt, leans on the door frame, stares at me. Leukon. A specter that once was Leukon. We remain silent for a long time, until I can whisper: Arethusa? He nods, pushes himself off the door frame, lurches away in the direction of the hall where they're holding the tribunal.

Probably some more time has passed. Now the great doors of the hall are being opened. Now the messenger who's been waiting outside the door for his entrance is receiving his instructions. Now he sets off, comes closer. Now I'm seized by a longing for all the days they'll rob me of. For all the sunrises. For meals with the children, for Oistros's embraces, for the songs that Lyssa sings. For all the simple joys, which are the only ones that last. Now I've left them all behind me.

The messenger is here.

Nine

Jason

JASON:
For it were better for mortals to get
children
From some other source, and for
there to be
No female sex. Then mankind
would have no trouble.

EURIPIDES, *Medea*

I didn't want any of this to happen. But what could I have done? She brought this disaster on herself. The lunatic. She wanted to show me. She was determined to crush me. And even if they should hack her into pieces, there would still be her eyes. Which won't stop staring at me.

From the very first moment when the messenger led her into the hall, she was searching only for me. She found me, forced me to my feet by her gaze alone. As though they were going to pronounce sentence on me too. She didn't look at the King's spokesman, she had eyes only for me. She was raising her brazenness to a new level, but, after all, what did she have to lose.

It wouldn't have made the slightest difference if I had played the bigmouth and defended her before the Council. With what, may I ask. And for what reason. That she hadn't taken part in poor Turon's humiliation, but indeed had helped to rescue him? Nobody would have bought that one. They would have barred me from the hall too. As it was, they were certainly paying close attention to the way I behaved.

Gods. Those demented Colchian women. To cut the man's sex off. All of us, all of the men in Corinth, shared in his pain. During the nights that preceded the Colchian women's punishment and Medea's conviction, you can be absolutely certain that no child was begotten and no man capable of begetting one. They came down hard on their wives—it's said that many a husband beat his—and now the Corinthian women hide themselves in their houses or run through the streets with bowed heads, as though they, each one of them, had mutilated poor Turon. They flatter their men and give a full-throated welcome to the harsh punishments inflicted on the guilty Colchians and demand the supreme penalty for Medea, and the loudest, as usual, are those who owe her thanks. And when these evil times are finally over and we all get some peace again, then the men of Corinth will be on top and the women even further down and that'll be the end of the story.

It should be all right with me, but it's not all right with me. Nothing pleases me anymore. She predicted it. Not crowing or showing off, no, more like sad, or sympathetic, which was pretty impertinent. She herself had lost all chance for sympathy through her own folly. That was said to me in the Council when I tried to beg some leniency for her, while at the same time not failing to emphasize the gravity of her offense (otherwise they would have ripped me to shreds). Akamas chose to rub my nose in the matter of my relationship with Medea, he was so very understanding, he spoke to me man-to-man, and I stood there like an ox and didn't blink an eye as he, the worthy Akamas, hinted that her chief distinction no doubt lay in her abilities as a woman, and who would reproach me for taking advantage of those. But because of that, naturally I'm prejudiced in her favor. I would have liked to strike him in the face. Instead of which I sat down and scarcely even raised my eyes again, to say nothing of any attempts at further speechifying. Besides, everything was already decided. They were speaking the parts written for them. The verdict was certain. I don't know why they needed all this playacting. They even pretended to take it seriously.

So why did I go to see her yet again. Why didn't I spare myself that. She was busy packing her things. She hardly looked up. Ah, Jason, she said. Am I supposed to provide you with a clear conscience? All I wanted to do was explain to her how things had gone and assure her that someone like me couldn't have done anything. She laughed out loud. Someone like you, she said, who's about to be given the King's daughter for a wife. But let me tell you something, Jason, don't you do anything to Glauce. She loves you, you know, and she's fragile, very fragile. Of course, she's not a Queen by any means, and you, my dear Jason, you're no King for Corinth, and that's the best thing I can say about you now. You won't take pleasure in it. Generally speaking, you won't take pleasure in very much anymore. Things are so arranged that not only those who must suffer injustice but also those who do injustice have miserable lives. As a matter of fact, I wonder whether the enjoyment of destroying other people's lives doesn't come from a person's having so little enjoyment and pleasure in his own.

She talked like that, and I grew more and more enraged. A man takes the risk of disregarding strict prohibitions, and then he finds himself lumped together with the shadowy figures around Akamas, with that indomitably vain Presbon, for example, who was summoned to appear before the Council as a witness and who simply didn't know how to curb his pomposity. I hadn't seen him in a long time, and I was repelled by the way his features have collapsed. He was ready to say anything against Medea. The members of the Council could sit back at their contemptuous ease and listen while all manner of vileness and obscenities were hurled at the accused by one of her own countrymen. That sort of talk isn't usually heard in the palace. The foolish fellow thought he could permit himself every liberty, they let him bluster on to his heart's content, and only when he was in the process of expressing his outrage at Medea for stopping the Corinthians from killing the prisoners in the temple did Akamas cut him off—Enough!—and he clapped his foolish mouth shut. He'd done his duty. His time is about to come to an end, he just doesn't know it. I, however, have been close to the King, and I've learned to read the signs.

Agameda's a different case. She's cleverer than Presbon. The royal house of Corinth couldn't have wished for a more convincing witness against Medea, precisely because Agameda didn't let herself drop so much as a single word of suspicion, to say nothing of accusation, against her mortal enemy. Against my will, I had to admire her. She managed to hide the fact that she hates Medea, that she's her rival as long as she lives inside the walls of this city. I realized that there isn't enough room in Corinth for both these women. Agameda would have spoken in favor of stoning Medea if there hadn't been the possibility of banishment, which is, often enough, the equivalent of a death sentence anyway. I saw her cold, bloodthirsty eyes while she, looking quite self-controlled, was sketching a picture of how Medea lived her life and what she was up to in Corinth, a picture with a very strong resemblance to the Medea we know, except that she gave such a new interpretation to Medea's every action, her every omission, that at the end there emerged before our eyes a person who for a long time had been pursuing the downfall of the Corinthian royal house. Once I had to laugh out loud, when she called Medea's caring for Glauce a particularly perfidious means of achieving her goal. The looks I got from the others after that taught me how inappropriate my laughter had been. Glauce, sitting next to me, didn't change expression. And I lost heart for laughing when Agameda declared that Medea had made use of me too; in order to penetrate into the inner circle around the royal family, she'd let me believe that she was my wife and I was her husband, while in fact she'd been satisfying her needs elsewhere for a long time. I sat there, feeling mighty small, and had to listen to the name of Medea's lover, because Agameda had an answer to every query, and for every assertion that she made she kept ready in her head the necessary names and a description of the exact circumstances. She's a murderous bitch, and my dislike of her grew along with my admiration. So it's Oistros. A stonecutter. Gods.

As though by coincidence and in passing, Agameda had casually tossed almost every member of the Council a remark, a name, a suspicion connected to Medea, something he could gnaw on that made him incapable even of thinking anything in her favor, as I was. When she was finally led into the room, the only thing I felt was rage. Now, before all the people, I was the deceived husband, instead of her being the abandoned wife the way she should have been. She got what she deserved, the whore.

Banishment.

Yes. Not at all excessive. Did she turn pale? I didn't look at her.

And the children?

She stirred a bit, sought my eyes again, but she was not going to find them.

Without the children, Creon said.

It was the only time that he himself spoke. Jason's children would be brought up in Corinth, in a manner befitting their station. In the palace.

I saw her totter, but she caught herself before the guards could take hold of her.

To everyone's amazement, Agameda and Glauce argued in support of letting her take the children with her. They each had different reasons for doing this. Although, now that I stop to think about it, the two of them had one reason in common: they didn't want Medea's sons ever to come into consideration as possible candidates for the Corinthian throne. But who's to say that I'll get this poor Glauce pregnant if she becomes my wife? It's not exactly foaming lust that seizes me when I feel her bones through her shapeless black clothing. I saw Agameda's disparaging look stray from me to Glauce, I saw that Glauce saw that look and that she understood it exactly the same way I did, and then I heard her speak. Her voice was indeed low, but her speaking at all before this male assembly was unprecedented.

We should let the mother take her children with her, she said. We should not be needlessly cruel. That was really her opinion, I'm sure of it. It's just that behind this opinion loomed her uncertainty whether she would be capable of giving Corinth an heir, and that it was only this insecurity that gave her the courage to speak out against cruelty. I began to suspect that perhaps this Glauce wouldn't be such a convenient wife as I had hoped after all, in any case I was distracted and didn't pay close attention to the sentence with which Akamas, speaking in a tone of forbearance, dismissed the suggestion of the two women the way one refuses children some unreasonable request. Then there occurred a minor incident that few people noticed: Leukon, who had come late and looked considerably the worse for wear, arose from his seat near the door and simply left the hall. It took incredible cheek to do this, it showed contempt for the King and for all the rules. But no one appeared to give it a second thought.

Medea was led away. The King and his retinue left the hall. Rigid spines, blank faces. I followed with Glauce. She was crying. As we were crossing the palace courtyard and approaching the well, she began to twitch, her arms flailed in the air, and she collapsed next to me with foam on her mouth. Agameda was at her side at once, as though she'd been waiting for the fit to come. My skull was bursting. What have I let myself in for?

I ran through the city, people got out of my way, suddenly I was standing in front of the little house on the palace wall. Lyssa tried to prevent me from entering, but Medea said, Let him pass. She asked, What do you want now? Her tone made me angry. I wanted her to see that she was wrong. I wanted her to admit that I couldn't have helped her. She tied up her bundle. She bound a cloth around her head. She said, It's a shame about you, Jason.

That was too much. I didn't have to take that. I could act differently. Give in to my rage. Jump on her and shove her against the wall. No one insults Jason and gets away with it. She had to realize that Jason can work up some fine manly fury against cheap female tricks, he can become quite strong when he feels the soft flesh he's dug his nails into give way under him, when he finally sees something like surprise in a woman's eyes before she closes them and turns her head aside and lets the inevitable happen. Yes. I understood. That's the way it's meant to be. We should take women. We should break down their resistance. That's the only way to root out what nature has endowed us with, the vile lust that spills over everything.

Not a look, not one word more. I went away. I never saw her again.

Ten

Leukon

In some respects, the planet is like
the *Argo:* purposeless, on an
irrelevant mission, exposed to the
finite adventures of time.

DIETMAR KAMPER

*H*ere they come leaping out again, my constellations. How I hate these dreary repetitions. How loathsome all this is to me. I cannot say that to anyone, but it is also the case that there is no longer anyone who would want to hear it. So I sit here alone and drink wine and watch the movements of the stars. And I must see the images again and again, whether I want to or not, must hear the voices that haunt me. I did not know what a human being could endure. Now I sit here, obliged to tell myself that it is this ability to bear what is unbearable and to go on living, to go on doing what one is used to doing—it is this uncanny ability that the existence of the human species is based on. If I said this previously, I did so in the words of a spectator, for a man is a spectator as long as there is no other person close to him, as long as no one else's misfortune can break his heart. Of all the unnamed stars in the heavens, I have named the brightest one Arethusa, and every time it sets in the western sky, as it is doing now, I feel the same pain. Among all these distant worlds I am alone in my world, and I like it less the better I know it. And understand it, I cannot deny that. As much as I search my heart, and as little as I wish to admit what that search reveals, I cannot find that there was a single one of the recent atrocities—and I was a witness to them—where I did not understand both sides. Not that I excuse them, no, but I understand. Humans in their blindness. This compulsion to understand seems to me like a stigma that I cannot get rid of and that isolates me from other people. Medea knew about such things.

How can I forget that last look she cast toward me as the two guards who were holding her by the arms expelled her from my city of Corinth through the southern gate, after she had been led, as is customary with scapegoats, through the city streets, which were lined by a hate-frothing, screaming, spitting, fist-shaking mob? And I (who would believe me?), I felt something like envy for this dirty, besmirched, exhausted woman, who was banished from the city with a shove from the guards and a curse from the High Priest. Envy, because she, the innocent victim, was free from inner conflict. Because the rift did not run through her, but gaped between her and those who had slandered and condemned her, who drove her through the city, insulted her, spat upon her. So that she could pick herself up out of the filth into which they had shoved her, could raise her arms toward Corinth and with all that remained of her voice announce that Corinth is doomed. Those of us who were standing near the gate heard this threat and walked without speaking back into the deathly still city, which seemed empty to me without the woman. But together with the burden that Medea's fate laid upon my heart, I felt pity for the Corinthians, these pathetic, misguided wretches, who could not otherwise free themselves from their fear of the plague and of the ominous signs in the heavens and of hunger and of the palace's encroachment upon their lives than by shifting their fear onto that woman. Everything is so transparent, everything is so clear and obvious, it can make one crazy.

The plague is abating, it has already withdrawn from the wealthier districts of the city, before darkness falls I look out from my tower and see at most one or two corpse carts still moving in the direction of the necropolis. Now everyone can see that we correctly interpreted the will of the gods when we drove the sorceress out of the city. I say "we," almost without flinching. We the Corinthians. We the just. Even I did nothing to save her. I am a Corinthian. It is better to acknowledge it, better to wallow in the grief and shame that drive me up to this tower night after night. In order to think the thought that can make me lose my reason: had Arethusa lived, she would not want me anymore. I shall learn to live with this truth too, I know it. And I shall not jump to my death from up here, no matter how often I stand on the terrace wall and look down. I have always taken care to preserve myself from bodily harm. That is the way we are made, there must be some sense in it. And sometimes I ask myself what gives a person, what gave that woman, the right to confront us with decisions that we are not equal to making, decisions that tear us apart and leave us feeling inferior, incompetent, guilty.

Why can I not be like Oistros. Oistros works in his cavelike workshop like a man possessed; he has barricaded himself in there and will grant admittance to no one. He neglects himself, never washes, lets his beard and his red hair grow wild, hardly eats, drinks water out of the enormous pitcher that used to stand in Arethusa's room, and hammers at a great massive block of stone with a fury that frightens me. He does not speak, stares at me with eyes inflamed by stone dust and sleeplessness. I do not even know if he recognizes me at all. He himself has changed beyond recognition. If he should step into the street, children would scream and run away from him. I do not know what he wants to extract from his stone. The last time I saw it, I thought I could make out suggestions of figures vehemently embracing, limbs in a kind of hopeless struggle, each against each, or in their death throes. One cannot ask. He is working himself to death. It is what he wants.

Oistros has lost all sense of moderation, just as Medea, too, had lost all sense of moderation. She was immoderate at the end, a Fury, just what the Corinthians needed her to be. The way she forced an entry into the Temple of Hera, holding the pale frightened boys by the hand, and pushed aside the priestess who stepped in front of her; the way she led the children to the altar and shouted out to the goddess what sounded more like a threat than a prayer: she, the goddess, must protect these children, since she, the mother, could no longer do so. The way she obligated the priestesses to look after the children, which they promised to do out of pity and fear. The way she talked to the children then, tried to calm their anxiety, embraced them, and, without even looking around, left the temple and immediately turned herself over to the waiting guards. The way she sang out, the whole time she was being led like a scapegoat through the city, a horrible song that goaded the people along the way into trying to stifle it. She must have been determined to be killed, but the guards had been ordered to get her out of the city alive.

Later, after the appalling thing had happened, they sent out commandos to find Medea. They searched for Lyssa, who had disappeared as well; they interrogated the few surviving Colchians under torture in an attempt to beat out of them the whereabouts of the two women. But it seemed, and seems, as though the earth had swallowed them up, even though one must walk for days beyond the city walls before finding any sort of hiding place. Now they are looking for accomplices who might possibly have helped the two get away on horseback, but this is only make-work, designed to avoid admitting that they are powerless and cannot avenge the death of the King's daughter. Moreover, they wish to nip in the bud the legends that are emerging already among the superstitious people: that the Goddess Artemis herself freed the fugitives from the earth in her snake-chariot and carried them off to safer regions.

Poor Glauce. It was the day of Medea's expulsion. I was crouching as though drugged in a corridor of the palace. Women's cries surged up from the palace courtyard, I paid them no heed. I had contempt for everything that had anything to do with this royal house. I began to take notice only when I saw Merope, the old Queen, leaning on her maidservants and dragging herself across the courtyard, all the way to the well, around which the throng of screaming women had formed a circle. Then I saw the throng move apart, saw three servants with a rope hoisting a strange burden, all dressed in white, out of the well: Glauce.

They placed her lifeless form at the Queen's feet. I saw her kneel down and lay her daughter's head in her lap. She remained in that position for a long time, and little by little a stillness descended, the likes of which I had never heard in that place. I felt as though that silence hid within itself something like grief and justice for all the victims that people in their blindness leave behind them in this labyrinth. All was still, and then I saw Jason totter across the court-yard as though someone had given him a blow to the head. No one turned around to look at him. They say that now he sleeps under the half-rotted hulk of his ship, which has been raised up onto trestles near the shore, and Telamon, his old companion, provides him one way or another with food and drink. Sometimes in the depths of the night I think that he cannot sleep either, that his eyes, too, are scanning the heavens, and his gaze and mine could meet by chance in the constellation of Orion, which dominates the zenith this month. I can feel no resentment against Jason. He was too weak for an opponent like Akamas.

Who is now in complete control. It was he who put out the report about Glauce's death, and whoever contests his version is as good as dead. Medea is supposed to have sent Glauce a poisoned dress, a gruesome farewell gift, and as poor Glauce was putting it on, it burned her skin so badly that the pain drove her mad, and she threw herself into the well to cool her scorched flesh.

Now this palace is indeed a place with a hundred ears and a

hundred mouths, and all of them whisper something different. The mouth of poor Glauce's maid, who is locked in a deep dungeon and carefully guarded, whispers: That white dress, which Medea wore to the Festival of Artemis, she gave to Glauce as a gift shortly before the trial, telling her that it was meant to be her wedding dress and wishing her luck, and Glauce, in tears, thanked her for the gift. But then, when she came out of the courtroom, after Medea's sentence had been pronounced and her expulsion was drawing ever closer, Glauce became visibly more uneasy. She went wandering through the palace and several times had to be flushed out of and brought back from one of the remote corners she had crawled into. She did not want to see Jason at any price, and she shrank away from Creon with every indication of horror. She spoke only to herself, in a hurried, unintelligible manner. She seemed utterly distracted; no one could know how much she still comprehended. She refused food as though she found it revolting. Nobody told her about what was going on outside the palace, that was strictly forbidden, but she had an instinct for it, and on the day when Medea was expelled from the city Glauce kept running back and forth in her room, wringing her hands and weeping. At last she called for the white wedding dress to be brought to her and put it on despite the maid's objections. Then all at once she became quite calm, as though she now knew what she had to do. Speaking reasonably, she told the maid that she wanted to get a bit of air in the palace courtyard, a request that could but gladden the hearts of all those assigned to guard her. So she walked into the courtyard ahead of the maid and a few guards, and she cunningly led them in ever-narrowing circles until she was near the well. Two quick steps, and she was standing on its rim. Then a further step into the void, into the depths. The maid says she did not make a sound.

As for the King, nobody has seen him since then. He is said to be lying low in the innermost of his chambers, and only Akamas is admitted into his presence. He is a dead man. Behind his back, the struggle for the succession is beginning. It leaves me cold. Nor am I curious about what further machinations Akamas will resort to in order to maintain his influence. Naturally he must try to blot out remembrance. Presbon and Agameda, his accomplices, have been got out of the city by his orders. He has had the entrance to the cave tomb of Iphinoe, with whose death all this began, walled up. Merope, the old Queen, is under house arrest. Whoever has been a witness to Akamas's maneuvers must be in fear for his life. Including me. On the day when poor Glauce met her death, he let me know how things stood. We were facing each other across her bier. Something or other in my look made him shudder. It is this shudder that protects me, along with my indifference to my fate. The fact that I see all the way through people, including him, protects me, and it is just for this reason, strange as it may sound, that I am not dangerous. Since I do not believe that I or anyone else can change them, I shall not interfere with the murderous processes that they keep in motion. No, I sit here and drink the wine that I drank with Medea, and I spill a few drops from each glass in memory of the dead. It is enough for me to watch the stars moving in their predictable courses and to wait until the pain gradually loosens its grip. So the morning comes, the city awakens, always with the same movements, always with the same sounds, and so shall it remain, let happen what may. The people in their cramped houses will return to their everyday lives. Some of them have engendered a child in the night, that is as it should be, that is why they are there.

But here is something out of the ordinary. A crowd of people is coming from the direction of the temple compound. I move to the railing. They are already gathering in the square, a crowd in a victorious mood. What could they have to celebrate? A buzzing comes from them, they sound to me like a swarm of attacking bees. My hands become moist, something drives me down among these people. They are still agitated, they cannot disperse, they remain thronged together and boast about what they have done. The crowd surges this way and that; I run from one group to another, I want to hear what they are talking about, but I dare not understand them. It had to be, I hear them declare that again and again. For a long time it had been clear to them, they say, that they would be unable to tolerate this any longer. Since nobody else was willing to do it, they had to do it themselves.

Through the veil that hangs over my eyes, I see Akamas's new familiar coming into the square, a rough, wily fellow. Through the roaring of the heartbeat in my ears, I hear him ask what is going on, but he asks as if he knows the answer. The crowd falls silent, then several of them call out: We've done it. They're gone. Who, the fellow asks. The children! is the answer. Her goddamned children. We've freed Corinth from that pestilence. And how? asks the fellow, with a conspiratorial expression on his face. Stoned them! many voices bellow. As they deserved.

The sun is coming up. How the towers of my city gleam in the morning light.

Eleven

Medea

Men, who are excluded from the
mystery of bringing forth life, find
in death a power which, since it
takes life away, is considered the
mightier of the two.
ADRIANA CAVARERO, *In Spite of Plato*

D*ead*. They murdered them. Stoned them, Arinna says. And I had thought their vindictiveness would pass if I went away. I didn't know them.

She didn't recognize me, but she knew Lyssa, her mother, from a dark brown mark on the inside of her elbow. How shocked she was. Our life here has changed us. The caves. The merciless summer sun, the winter cold. The lichen, the beetles, the insects and snails and ants that serve as our food. We are the shadows of our former years.

We were blind. We would speak of the children as though they were alive. We pictured them growing up, year after year. They were to be our avengers. And I had not yet got past the outskirts of their city when they were already dead.

What fiend led Arinna here? Will the gods teach me to believe in them again? I can only laugh. I'm sick of them now. Wherever they may probe me with their cruel instruments, they will find in me no trace of hope, no trace of fear. Nothing, nothing. Love is shattered, even pain stops. I am free. Desiring nothing, I hark to the void, which fills me utterly.

And the Corinthians, it seems, are not through with me yet.

What do they say? That I, Medea, murdered my children. I, Medea, wanted to revenge myself on Jason. Who's going to believe that, I ask. Everybody, Arinna says. Even Jason? He has nothing more to say. But the Colchians? They're all dead, except for the women in the mountains, and they have turned savage.

Arinna says that in the seventh year after the children's death the Corinthians selected seven boys and seven girls from noble families. Shaved their heads. Sent them into the Temple of Hera, where they must remain for a year in commemoration of my dead children. And this is to be done from now on, every seven years.

That's the way it is. That's what it has come to. They're at pains to assure that even posterity will call me a child-murderess. But what will that mean to them, compared with the horror that they'll look back on? For we are not teachable.

What is left to me. To curse them. My curse upon you all. My curse especially upon you: Akamas. Creon. Agameda. Presbon. May a hideous life be your lot, and a miserable death. May your howling mount up to heaven and leave it unmoved. I, Medea, put my curse on you.

Where can I go. Is it possible to imagine a world, a time, where I would have a place. There's no one I could ask. That's the answer.